# WINTER CAMP

# WINTER CAMP

## Kirkpatrick Hill

SCHOLASTIC INC.
New York Toronto London Auckland Sydney

ISBN 0-590-20518-8

Copyright © 1993 by Kirkpatrick Hill. All rights reserved. Published by Scholastic Inc., 555 Broadway, New York, NY 10012, by arrangement with Viking Penguin, a division of Penguin Books USA Inc.

12 11 10 9 8 7 6                              5 6 7 8 9/9 0/0

Printed in the U.S.A.                                    40

First Scholastic printing, February 1995

*For* JOHN MINOOK HARPER

✳✳ *with love* ✳✳

## ✳✳ 1 ✳✳

TOUGHBOY AND SISTER HAD LIVED JUST like most of the other kids along the Yukon River. There was fish camp in the summer, moose hunting in the fall, school in the winter, good times, bad times, everything the way it usually is in Alaskan villages.

Then things began to happen to them, and their lives changed. First Mamma died, with the new baby. Then Daddy died the next year and they were all alone, except for Mutt.

They went to live with Natasha that fall, after Daddy died.

The old house where they'd lived with Mamma and Daddy was next door to Natasha's. The doors and windows were boarded over with plywood now that no one lived there, and dingy yellow birch leaves covered the front step.

When Toughboy and Sister looked at that house it was hard to believe that they'd once lived in it. Everything seemed so long ago.

But Mutt would sometimes go to their old house and whine and scratch at the door, just as if he thought Mamma or Daddy would open it.

Mutt was the last dog from Daddy's old dog team. He'd been the leader and he was older than Toughboy.

Most people in their village would have gotten rid of such an old dog, but even though Natasha was a grouchy sort of person she never grumbled about Mutt. She even let him sleep in the house because he was so old. Sister thought that Natasha and Mutt were friends because she was old, too.

Natasha was the oldest person in the village and she knew how to do everything. She could hunt and trap, and make mittens and mukluks, and work on an outboard motor, and train dogs. She could make snowshoes and rawhide and smoked fish strips.

She was just about the last person in their

village who knew how to do these things. No one wanted to learn the old ways anymore.

Natasha said people were lazy now. "Kyuh," she'd say, in the hard Indian way, almost spitting out the word. "They just get them checks from the government and don't do nothing. Sitting around doing nothing. And drinking all the time. There's no Indians left."

When Natasha talked like that Toughboy would want more than anything to be a good Indian. He wanted to learn all the old ways. He wondered if Natasha had thought his father was a good Indian.

He didn't think so.

Toughboy was almost twelve. He had straight black hair that fell into his eyes all the time, and he was skinny and short for his age. Not much to look at, Natasha always said, in case he was getting full of himself.

Sister was two years younger, and she always looked serious, so she seemed to be much older than she was.

Their real names were John and Annie Laurie Silas, but no one ever called them that. Most Athabascan children were called by nicknames.

Natasha said that was because children in the old days weren't named until they were grown up. So they just had a joking name or a baby name until they were bigger.

Natasha told them her baby name. It was a long, singing word in Indian that sounded like making fun of something.

Natasha had never had any children of her own. Toughboy and Sister were the first children who had ever lived with her.

She wasn't easy to live with.

They had a hard time learning to do the chores the way Natasha wanted them done. She was very impatient, and her face would grow cold and stern if they couldn't learn something right away. Sister remembered how slowly and carefully Mamma would explain things. It was easy to understand when Mamma showed her how.

Worst of all was when Natasha would say, disgusted, "Didn't your mom and dad teach you *nothing?*" There was no answer to that. They hated it when she blamed Mamma and Daddy for the things they didn't do right, and so they tried very hard to please her.

But she wasn't always cross.

On fall evenings, when it had begun to get dark early, Natasha would knit and sew and fix things. Toughboy and Sister would sit with her and do their schoolwork, and Mutt would lie on the rug by the door where it was the coolest, and watch them, his chin stretched out on his paws.

There were photographs all over the wall, family pictures. Every house that Toughboy and Sister had ever been in had family pictures hanging everywhere, and sitting in frames on the tables and dressers.

Most of Natasha's family pictures were very old. The frames were fancy, and the pictures in them were brown and soft-looking. There was a gold name at the bottom of some of the pictures. Natasha said that was the name of the man who had taken the picture.

In the old days, when the village had been a big mining town, a traveling photographer had come, and he'd taken pictures of everyone in Natasha's family. There was a picture of her mother in a beautiful fox parka, and of Natasha and her little sisters dressed in high button shoes and long dresses very tight at the waist.

Sister would look hard at Natasha's brown and

wrinkled face to find the little girl in the pictures. But she couldn't. Just the eyes were still there, black and bright and ornery-looking.

There were pictures of Natasha grown up, too. Toughboy's favorite was one of Natasha and her husband at their trapline. Between them they held a long pole, and from the pole hung nearly a hundred marten skins. Natasha said she had taken the picture herself, and she showed them the string she had been holding in her hand to click the camera shutter.

Sister would touch the cool glass on the pictures and stare hard at the faces there. She wanted to know what those people were like, what their voices sounded like. But they stayed frozen in those frames and didn't move.

When she asked Natasha their names Natasha would tell stories about those people as she worked.

They were wonderful stories, and Toughboy and Sister would forget what they were doing and would sit without moving, big-eyed, watching Natasha's face as she talked.

She told them how her grandmother had killed a bear with a spear. "She was a beautiful woman," said Natasha. Sister looked closely again at the picture on the wall of the old bent woman, so ugly she looked like the drawing of a witch in a storybook. Then Sister looked at Natasha to see if she was joking about the beautiful part, but Natasha had her faraway look, and wasn't joking at all.

Natasha suddenly closed her eyes and began to sing an Indian song. Then she quit abruptly and opened her eyes. "That's her song that they made for her at potlatch. But I forgot the rest. Those songs are lost, all lost."

Natasha told them how her father had given her baby brother away to a medicine man. And at the medicine man's camp that baby brother had fallen into a vat of boiling dog feed and had died terribly.

There was a cousin who was born all crooked and had to be carried in a sling everywhere the family went.

There was the story of Natasha's grandfather who had come home one day with two new wives, and how her grandmother had been so mad that she'd gone off into the woods with her six children and had built her own underground house.

Sister thought what Mamma would have done if Daddy had come home with two new wives.

Natasha said in those days some men had more than one wife, but usually they were the medicine men, because only the medicine men would be rich enough to keep more than one wife.

Medicine men got rich because they made the other people give them what they wanted. People were afraid of them. That's why Natasha's father had given that baby away. Sister thought they sounded cruel and awful, those medicine men.

Each story Natasha told was better than the last.

## 2

BESIDES THE STORIES, NATASHA TOLD them about the special way things must be done, and the things they must never do or say. There were a million of those.

If a thing was wrong, it was *hutlanee*. You must never say you were going hunting for such and such an animal. It was *hutlanee* to say the name of the animal. If you did, the spirit of the animal would hear and wouldn't let itself be caught. If you were going hunting all you could say was, "I'm going to have a little look around."

You must not throw away the bones of the animal after it was killed. That was *hutlanee*. You must bury the bones and say some Indian words. This was so the animal's spirit wouldn't be offended. Natasha knew a lot of stories about people who hadn't caught a bear or a beaver in many, many years because they had done the wrong things. The animal had to *let* you catch it.

You couldn't be too careful in the old ways.

Daddy used to make fun of Mamma when she said something was *hutlanee*. He didn't believe in any of the old ways.

Mamma was careful about some things. She wouldn't eat bear meat or even look at a bear if she could help it, and she put food and cigarettes in the stove if they dropped on the floor. She said that meant the dead were hungry or wanted to smoke, so she put those things in the stove for them.

One night Toughboy asked Natasha about woodsmen. "Have you ever seen one?" he asked.

Natasha smiled unpleasantly. "Oh, some people say there's no such thing, but they don't know nothing. We seen their signs lots of times."

"But did you ever see one, truly see one?" asked Toughboy again.

"Maybe not," she snapped, "but I know lots of people who did. Mamma seen one on that hill behind their spring camp. He had eyes like a moose, she said, big eyes like this." Natasha made circles with her fingers to show how big the eyes were. "And long hair. All over his body. They're bigger than we are, maybe seven feet tall."

Toughboy felt his stomach grow hard with fear. "What do woodsmen do, Natasha?"

She frowned hard at her knitting. "They steal kids from people and they steal women. One summer there's one near us at fish camp. I hear all the time, off in the woods, someone shooting, shooting. That's him. He just shoots in the air."

Toughboy sat silent for a minute, imagining the eerie sound of aimless shooting coming from the dark woods. Then a question occurred to him.

"Where would woodsmen get their bullets, Natasha?"

She gave him such a hard look he was sorry he'd asked her.

The more Natasha talked to them about the old ways, the more mixed up Toughboy got.

He asked Dandy about it. Dandy had been away to Vietnam. He'd been a marine. On his mother's dresser there was a picture of him in a dark uniform and a white hat. Toughboy always saved hard questions for Dandy because he thought Dandy was the smartest person he knew.

He asked Dandy if owls really talked in Indian, and if there were really woodsmen who would steal you. Dandy laughed. "Don't listen to them old people. They're just superstitious. They don't know nothing."

When Dandy said that, Toughboy could see in his mind those long-ago people in Natasha's pictures looking sadly down at the village. They were left out and didn't belong anymore.

Thinking about the old ways that no one wanted anymore made Toughboy sad. It was sad to be old and not wanted. He'd like to be a good Indian and learn the old ways.

But some of the old things Natasha told them were scary.

Natasha wouldn't let them look out of the windows into the dark. *"Hutlanee,"* she said. "Don't look out." When Toughboy asked why, she frowned fiercely. "You get bad luck that way," she said. "Just do what I tell you."

Toughboy knew she was talking about the ghosts that would try to take you with them to where the dead people lived. Nearly everyone believed in ghosts and a lot of people had seen one.

Thinking of ghosts made Toughboy nervous when he had to go to the outhouse in the dark.

## ✳✳ 3 ✳✳

THE HARD BRIGHT DAYS OF FALL WERE
over and the trees were bare.

Sister thought everything looked ugly when
the leaves were gone. She waited for the first snow
to bury the junky machinery and trash in the
yards and the muddy, rutted roads.

The clean snow finally came, tumbling slowly
out of the soft gray sky, softening the hard edges
of the town.

Natasha stood on the porch with her arms
folded, watching the snow fall. When she came
back into the house, stamping the snow off her
feet, she had a shining look that they'd never seen
on her face before.

"I'm going to take you to the trapline," she said.

14

They looked at her with surprise, so she scowled. "What's the matter, you think I'm too old to go trapping?"

They shook their heads fast to show that they'd never thought such a thing, but Natasha was still mad at them. "I can walk circles around you on snowshoes, and anyone else in this town. Nobody can't snowshoe like me."

She'd show Toughboy and Sister how to live off the land, so they wouldn't just sit around all the time like some people she could name. She'd take Toughboy and Sister to winter camp, and she'd show them how to do everything the old-time way. They were lucky to be living with her, Natasha, who could teach them the Indian ways.

Sister was worried.

She knew the teacher would be mad at them. She got a tight-lipped look when the parents took their kids moose hunting or to muskrat camp. She'd grimly pack up schoolwork for them to take, more work than they would have done in school.

And if they made mistakes after they came back she'd say what could they expect, if they didn't come to school?

They were studying Australia, too, and Sister was writing a report about kangaroos. She wanted to finish that very much, and she wanted to hear everything about that hot, hot place.

They would miss the Christmas play, and the Christmas singing she loved.

Most of all Sister was afraid that Natasha would make them leave Mutt behind. They'd have to leave him with someone else who would tie him up outdoors on a chain, and Mutt would hate that.

And besides he would miss them. They were his family.

She didn't dare ask Natasha. She knew it would be silly to take a big dog like that. There was no need for a dog at winter camp.

But how could she say good-bye to Mutt, even for just two months?

Oh, everything was different and hard, since Mamma and Daddy died.

But Toughboy was happier than Sister had ever seen him.

Every day he looked at the picture on the wall

of Natasha and her husband by the trapline cabin. Her husband had tall leather boots, laced all the way up to the knees, and a kind of squashed-up, old-time hat. He was really tough, you could see that. His eyes were twisted up hard in the sun and he had a cigarette in his mouth. There were snowshoes stuck in the snowbank by the cabin.

Toughboy thought of himself out there at that trapline, striding along tall and straight in snowshoes with a pack on his back. He would be the best trapper there ever was.

Wouldn't Daddy be proud if he could see him?

In the old days Natasha and her husband had gone out to the trapline with their dog team. Their cabin was on the Sulatna, a river a hundred and fifty miles away, so it would take them about three days to get there. They'd camp out at night on the way.

Then, when her husband died, Natasha went out with Mary Potter. There was a picture on the wall of Natasha and Mary, and they had a pole full of marten pelts longer than the one in the other picture.

Toughboy and Sister remembered Mary Potter, a very old lady who hardly spoke any English.

She would call out to them, *"Sakoyyaa!"*—
"grandchild"—when she saw them, and would
fish pieces of hard candy out of her pocket to give
to them. She had pieces of dry meat and smoked
salmon in that pocket, too, so the candy always
tasted strange.

Natasha said Mary Potter had frozen to death
after a potlatch. She had been drinking and had
fallen into a snowbank, and they didn't find her
until the next morning.

"Her own fault," Natasha said, crossly.

Natasha hadn't had a dog team since Mary
Potter died, so they'd fly to the trapline.

That was the best part. They were going out
in Billy Cross's Super Cub.

Toughboy had never flown in a small plane,
except once when they took him to Fairbanks
when he was a baby and had pneumonia. He
didn't remember that, of course.

He could hardly wait to fly with Billy.

Natasha had Sister write a letter to Billy Cross
to ask him to take them out at the end of October.

Billy ran the fuel depot in Tanana and flew
trappers to their lines every year. Then he'd pick
them up when the trapping season was over.

He was very forgetful, and there were lots of stories about Billy forgetting to pick up one of his trappers. Once, Joe Olson got tired of waiting for Billy and snowshoed all the way back to Tanana. When he got there he'd punched Billy in the nose for forgetting him.

Toughboy began to watch the gray skies anxiously. He listened to the radio report from Fairbanks every day.

To fly in the winter the weather had to be just right. There had to be just enough snow, but not too much. If it snowed too much they'd have to wait.

There had to be a good cold spell so there would be enough ice on the Sulatna to land a plane. If the ice wasn't thick enough they'd have to wait.

If it got too cold they'd have to wait.

Toughboy wouldn't be able to stand it if they had to wait.

# ✳ 4 ✳

FOR A WEEK NATASHA POKED THROUGH
the cache behind her house and dug out old snowshoes and axes and snare wire and lamp chimneys
for the gas lamps.

Natasha and Sister cut up a whole quarter of a
moose into thin pieces and hung them to dry in
the kitchen over the stove. That was dry meat.
Dry meat was chewy and tough and delicious.
You couldn't go trapping without it.

Natasha sent Toughboy to the fuel depot to
buy kerosene and white gas for the lamps, and
she sent Sister to the store for pilot crackers and
canned butter and boxes of dried apples, and a
dozen other things.

*　*　*

At the store Sister watched the last barge leave, going toward Nenana before the river froze up. The barge had delivered the liquor order for the store, and Manley, the store owner, had loaded up his big truck with cases and cases of beer. Five men had then formed a line with Manley and were passing the beer along from the truck to the store warehouse where extra food and beer was kept all winter.

Manley took time out to ring up Sister's groceries on the cash register and joked with her about going to the trapline. "Better not leave town, Sister. I might have to get a new girl-friend."

Sister just smiled at him. He always teased her.

"That Billy Cross is going to forget you out there. You'll miss Christmas, and Easter, too, the way that guy is!" Then he pinched her on the cheek. "I jokes," said Manley. That was down-river talk for "I'm only fooling."

There were too many packages for her to carry, so Sister left two of them at the store and ran home with the others. When she came back she heard music coming from the bar, sad October music for the gray day.

She stopped to listen. Someone was singing that song Daddy used to love. She walked to the open bar door and looked in. It was Freddy Pitka singing. He was pretty drunk. He saw her watching him and beamed. "Sister! Have a beer with me!" She giggled and waved her hand to say good-bye, and went back to get the other packages she'd left at the store.

Sister was beginning to feel lonesome for all the people in the village, and she hadn't even left yet.

Natasha patched the snowshoes and checked their clothes very carefully for holes and rips. She found two old canvas over-parkas with wolverine ruffs in the cache, and though they were much too big for Toughboy and Sister she was satisfied with them.

Soon there was a big pile of clothes and food and trapping equipment in the living room, and Sister couldn't imagine how all of it would fit in Billy's little plane.

"We have to make two trips," said Natasha.

Natasha packed everything carefully in small boxes and bundles because, she said, Billy could stick the boxes in the plane every which way if they were small, but there was no room for big boxes. It was the same as packing up a dog sled. You had to keep the bundles small.

Every night Sister would call Mutt onto her bed, after everyone had gone to sleep, and she'd smooth his ears and lean her face against his muzzle, trying to make up for the time she'd have to leave him. She hated to look at his trusting eyes.

Then the day before Billy was to pick them up, Natasha suddenly said, "Go out to the cache and get a piece of chain, Toughboy. We got to keep Mutt on a chain in the plane so he don't jump around."

So that was all right. Mutt would go with them. Sister didn't care about anything else. It didn't matter about school. It would only be two months, after all. And Mutt would go with them.

# 5

THE NEXT DAY, WHEN THEY WERE TO fly to the trapline, Toughboy woke while it was still dark and anxiously searched the black sky for signs of bad weather.

There were a few stars, and that meant it was clear. Just right.

He was so excited he couldn't eat the oatmeal Natasha cooked for breakfast. He felt as if there was a little scream caught inside his chest.

Long before anyone else heard a sound, Toughboy heard the tiny hum of Billy's Super Cub coming over the hills behind the village. In a few minutes Billy was buzzing the town in low circles. That was the signal that he was landing.

Natasha had asked Tony Arlo, who lived a few houses away, to help them get their things to the plane, so as soon as Toughboy heard the engine of the Super Cub he ran to Tony's. He and Tony drove up to the landing field with Tony's snow machine and big freight sled, and brought Billy down to Natasha's house.

Tony and Billy and Toughboy and Sister trudged in and out of the house, loading boxes and snowshoes and odd-shaped burlap bundles into the freight sled.

When Sister handed the box of schoolwork to Billy, Natasha took it out of his hands and set it back on the floor under the table. "We've got no room for that stuff," she snapped. "No time, anyway. This is a different kind of school you're going to now."

Sister and Toughboy looked at each other for a moment. Boy! Were they going to be in trouble when they got back. Toughboy smiled.

Sister thought of the three books she'd put in there. She'd wanted to read them so much. "But Natasha—" she started.

Natasha gave her one hard look. *"Dalek,"* she said. "Shut up."

* * *

In the end everything they'd packed did fit in the sled, but only half the sled load would fit in the plane.

Billy squinted at the four of them and decided. "I'll take you and the boy, then. Next load I'll get the girl and the dog." He jerked his chin at Sister.

Tony said that Mutt and Sister could wait at his house until Billy came back for the next load, so Natasha locked the door of her house and gave the key to Tony.

Sister took Mutt by the collar and walked through the snow to Tony's house while Tony took the sled and Natasha and Billy and Tough-boy up to the field.

Loading a little airplane was very complicated and had to be done just right. First Billy took the seat out of the back of the Super Cub and put it on the side of the runway. Now there would be room for two people. He would put the seat back in later when he picked up Sister and Mutt.

Then Billy tied the snowshoes to the struts of the plane so they would be out of the way.

Finally he stuffed Natasha and Toughboy and the little boxes here and there and everywhere.

The plane was piled to the roof with freight. Toughboy had to strain to see out of the side windows. There was a bundle of parkas for Natasha to sit on and she was leaning against a rolled-up sleeping bag, so she was all right, and she could see out of the window just fine. But Toughboy was crammed in with all the boxes, and there was an ax handle pushing hard against his ribs. It made him feel panicky to be jammed in so tight.

When Billy shut the door it gave a funny dull sound that made Toughboy feel as if the air in the plane was pushing tightly against his head.

Billy jumped into the front seat of the plane and started the engine. The motor sputtered and died and then caught and roared.

The noise was horrible and the whole plane shook violently. Toughboy suddenly knew that he was not going to like this ride.

As they taxied down the landing strip Toughboy could see Tony standing by his snow machine. He was shielding his eyes from the blizzard of snow raised by Billy's prop. Toughboy wished more than anything that he was standing there with Tony.

Natasha said something to Toughboy, but the roar of the engine was so loud he couldn't understand what she'd said. Faster and faster they went, and then with a little kick they were up in the air, and Toughboy could see the trees beneath them tilting sideways and growing smaller, smaller. Through the front window he saw the little village far beneath them, still asleep.

The roar of the engine and the smell of the gasoline were making Toughboy's head ache. Then stronger and stronger he could smell the dried fish in the burlap bag next to him. He thought of stories he'd heard of people who got sick in planes.

As soon as he thought of that he felt worse. An hour. He had to stay in this plane an hour. What if he threw up? He'd have to throw up on all the boxes. It would be so embarrassing. He just couldn't throw up.

This must be the worst feeling in the world. It was in his head and stomach and all his bones at the same time. He'd never, ever go up in a plane again. He'd *walk* back from the trapline.

Billy looked back over his shoulder to point out something on the ground to Natasha. She peered down with interest and then signaled Toughboy to look too. Toughboy closed his eyes. Leave me alone, he thought.

Billy reached back over his seat and handed Toughboy a paper bag. He was grinning. He thinks I'm going to be sick, Toughboy thought. Well, I'm not. And he shook his head to show that he didn't need the bag. Billy, still grinning, stuck the bag in a little pocket in the back of his seat and turned around.

Toughboy kept his eyes away from that bag, afraid to look at it, and tried to think of something else, anything else except the way he felt.

After forever had passed Toughboy heard a different sound in the engine and opened his eyes. Billy had slowed the plane down and was working the flaps. He was going lower and lower, looking intently out of the side window. Then there was a sliding sound and the skis bit into the snow on the river. Then Billy pushed the throttle forward again and the little plane climbed once more and turned sharply to one side. "Checking for overflow," Billy yelled to Natasha.

Toughboy's stomach fell against his heart and horrible slime climbed into his throat. Why couldn't Billy just fly this thing? Why did he have to go up and down and fast and slow and sideways?

It was no use. He was going to throw up.

Billy slowed down again for a landing and again the skis bit into the snow, but this time he didn't pull up again. The little plane hurtled down the river on its skis, snow flying up on all sides, and finally it came to a stop.

Toughboy kept his eyes shut, begging this to be the end. Then Billy shut off the engine and Toughboy knew it was all over. He opened his eyes as Billy jumped out of the cockpit and came around to the side to unfasten the door so Natasha and Toughboy could get out.

Toughboy's ears couldn't get used to the quiet after so much noise. He could hardly get to his feet, he was so cramped and miserable.

Billy helped Toughboy out of the plane and set him in the snow under the wing. Natasha climbed out afterward and she and Billy unloaded the plane, setting the boxes next to Toughboy in the snow.

Neither Billy nor Natasha looked as if they expected Toughboy to help them unload, and it was a good thing. Toughboy couldn't even hold his head up.

Then a soft wind blew across the river and washed Toughboy's face. The smell of the airplane, the dried-fish smell, and the gasoline smell all blew away and Toughboy began to feel better. He staggered out from beneath the wing and looked around him.

There, up on the bank, was the little cabin he'd seen in the old pictures on Natasha's wall. Tinier than he'd thought, it stood among tall, tall spruce trees. It was wonderful. It looked like home to Toughboy.

## ✳✳ 6 ✳✳

AFTER BILLY HAD TAKEN OFF AGAIN TO
pick up Sister and Mutt and the rest of their
things, Natasha unlocked the padlock on the
front door of the cabin.

"We never used to lock nothing in the old
days," she said. "Now everyone is stealing anything if you don't lock it up."

The door was hard to open and Natasha had to
swear at it and give it a hard kick. The old cabin
had been standing for nearly fifty years and it was
a little crooked. The doors didn't swing right,
now, and the windows had both cracked when
the house shifted.

Toughboy looked around him uncertainly. It

didn't look like much of a place to spend the winter in.

Natasha told Toughboy to get the hammer out of her bag and pull the plywood off the windows. When she and Mary had closed up the camp, Natasha had boarded up the windows so that bears couldn't get in.

Inside the cabin everything was dusty, and the light coming in through the cracked and smudged windows was dim.

But everything they needed was still in the cabin. There were snares and traps and saws and tools hanging neatly on nails hammered into the log walls. On the shelf over the door there was an old radio and a stack of stretchers for the skins of the animals they would trap.

Wood and kindling and birchbark tinder had been left by the stove. There were very old tin cans full of old-fashioned matches and mantles for the lamps. There was a Sir Walter Raleigh tobacco tin and a yellow can that read "KLIM, Milk spelled backwards."

When Billy came in a few hours later with Sister and Mutt, Toughboy was quite himself again.

He ran down to the plane to help Billy unload. He helped Sister get out of the plane and un-snapped the chain from Mutt's neck.

He looked carefully at Sister's face to see if she had been sick, too, but she seemed to be fine, digging into the plane to hand this and that to Toughboy.

Billy laughed at Toughboy. "Well, boy, your sister's a better flier than you are!" Sister looked at Toughboy to see what Billy meant. "Sicker than a dog," said Billy gleefully.

"I never threw up," Toughboy said sullenly.

"No, you sure didn't," admitted Billy. "It's better if you just throw up, you know," he said as he pulled the last box out of the plane. "I always feel better just as soon as I let it go."

Toughboy stared at Billy. "You mean you get sick, too?"

Billy laughed. "Every time it gets a little rough. I never could take much turbulence."

Toughboy felt better when he heard that. Still, he wished Sister had gotten sick instead of him. He helped Billy unload the rest of the boxes. He took the biggest boxes so Billy wouldn't think he was a sissy.

Natasha came down the bank and shook Billy's hand. "You be sure you come and get us on the twenty-second of December," she said. "You better not forget us."

"Now, Natasha, did I ever forget anyone?" And then he laughed because he knew he had. Natasha looked at him sourly.

"Don't worry," said Billy. "I'll have you home for Christmas. Be sure to listen to the radio then and I'll keep in touch."

They stood on the bank and watched until the little plane disappeared. In a few minutes they couldn't hear the sound of its engine anymore, and it was quiet, quiet, quiet. Quieter than fish camp in the summer because the snow muffled all the sounds. Winter camp.

Just like the old days.

## ✳✳ 7 ✳✳

ON THEIR WAY UP THE TRAIL TO THE
cabin, Toughboy and Sister stopped to laugh at
Mutt. He was like a windup toy, rushing crazily
here and there, nose down, bulldozing the snow,
ears up, smelling everything, without lifting his
head or stopping to take a breath.

It didn't seem possible his head could hold all
those smells at once.

When all the boxes and bundles had been brought
up from the river, Sister had time to look the
cabin over carefully.

There was a dirt roof, made of strips of tundra
moss.

There was a dirt floor, too.

In the old days people didn't put in boards for floors because the frozen ground under the house would heave and sink as it thawed out, and pretty soon the floor would be all wavy.

Sister wondered how you could keep a dirt floor clean.

A place in the corner was curtained off and that was where the washstand was. On the shelf over the washstand there was a piece of broken mirror. Sister stood on her tiptoes but she still couldn't see into the mirror.

Facing the door was a big wood stove made from an oil drum. Natasha's husband had welded a flat steel plate on the top so that you could cook on that stove. There were two wooden gas boxes next to the stove that were used as extra chairs.

A bunk bed made of spruce poles stood on the other side of the cabin. Natasha said the top bunk was for Toughboy and the bottom for Sister. There was another, wider bed along the same wall, and that was where Natasha would sleep.

Her bed had a metal headboard and footboard, and underneath the mattress there were rows of metal springs that squeaked when Natasha sat on the bed.

Natasha told Sister to lay the sleeping bags out on the beds. There were no pillows, but they could use their over-parkas and extra clothes for pillows if they wanted to.

In the afternoon the bright sun came leaking in through little cracks in the walls. Some of the old moss had dried up and fallen out from between the logs, so you could see daylight. That was bad, and you had to fill up those holes so the cold couldn't get in and the heat couldn't get out.

When they'd brought everything inside and had a good fire going, Natasha took them outside again to show them how to dig under the snow to find the kind of moss that they used to chink logs.

They stuffed all the holes full of that moss.

Natasha told them people had used moss for baby diapers in the old days. They carried their babies in little birchbark baskets with a strap between the babies' legs, and they would line that basket with moss to soak up the babies' urine.

Sister thought of that itchy moss next to a baby's bottom and she shuddered.

They found dried-up blueberries and cranberries under the snow when they were getting moss. They were left over from the summer. Natasha said that was what the shrews and other small animals lived on all winter, under the snow. But you must never eat them. That was *hutlanee*. If you did you would grow old and wrinkly, like the berries.

Natasha was so wrinkled that Toughboy wondered if she had ever eaten those berries, but he knew he'd better not ask.

When they finished with the moss, Natasha took a rusty plane off the wall and went to work on the stubborn door.

Soon she had a pile of curly shavings at her feet, and the door opened and shut easily again.

Natasha sent Sister to sweep out the outhouse, and then she showed them how to get water.

On the other side of the river, just across from the cabin, there was a good spot, away from sandbars. Black ravens wheeled over their heads and screamed with excitement while Natasha chopped a hole in the ice with the ice pick.

The ice was only three or four inches thick. She made the hole big enough so you could dip a whole galvanized bucket down into the water. Then she took a little shovel and cleared all the chipped ice out of the hole.

Every day they must chop the hole open again and clear the hole and then dip their buckets down into the river to get water. They'd melt snow, too, for extra water.

They would need just two buckets of water most days. The first bucket would fill the big kettle that always sat on the back of the stove, and the second they would put under the table for when they needed extra.

The water had tiny black bugs in it. Natasha said they were always there and they didn't need to pay any attention to them.

Sister tried to get the bugs out, anyway, when Natasha wasn't looking. But she could never get all of them out, and she thought the bugs made her food taste funny.

Next they put away the things in the boxes

they'd brought, and they washed the windows. They dusted and washed the things that had been hanging on the nails and sitting on the shelves. They'd brought too many things to keep in the little cabin, so they had to store the beans and the slab of bacon, the bait fish and coffee and flour in the cache behind the cabin.

The cache was like a little log house, about half as big as the cabin, and it stood on four tall spruce poles. It was built high in the air so that wild animals couldn't get into it. Sheets of tin were wrapped around the poles so that shrews and squirrels couldn't climb up to the cache and gnaw through the wooden door.

When you wanted to get something from the cache you had to use the ladder Natasha kept on top of the cabin roof. Toughboy and Sister liked climbing up and down that ladder, and they were glad every time Natasha found something else she wanted stored in the cache.

Then it was dark, and they lit the kerosene lamps and made a supper of canned Spam and rice and bannock. After she'd finished washing the dishes, Sister began to examine the old-fashioned cans and boxes in the cabin.

In a dark green Hills Brothers coffee can Sister found spruce pitch. Natasha said you could knock pitch off the trees with a stick during hard-crust time, when you could walk on the top of the snow. And then when you needed it you could boil it up with a little oil. You could patch up anything with pitch. Even people. If you put pitch on a bad cut it would heal up just right.

Sister thought about long ago when people had to get everything they needed from right here, from the woods and the tundra. She was glad she hadn't lived then.

# 8

FOR THE NEXT THREE DAYS THEY
worked to get the cabin ready for cold weather.
It was still warm in late October, not much below
zero, but there wasn't much time before winter
really set in.

First they would cut wood at the stand of
spruce not far from the cabin.

If Toughboy had been choosing the trees he
would have picked the little skinny ones. But
Natasha picked the big ones.

Natasha and Toughboy used the big swede saw
on those fat trees. Natasha held one end of the
saw and Toughboy the other, but she sawed so
fast and hard that she would jerk Toughboy off

his feet on the other end. No matter how he braced his feet and hung on, she would still yank him with every pull.

He hoped Sister and Natasha didn't notice.

Sister's job was to cut off the branches all along the trunks with the little ax.

She was very clumsy and slow at this, and Natasha and Toughboy had to help her get finished.

After the trees were limbed, Natasha and Toughboy sawed them into four-foot lengths and piled them on the toboggan. Later they would saw them in half so they'd fit in the stove. And then they'd split them with the ax.

Toughboy wished they'd brought the chain saw. He had never worked so hard in all his life. But Natasha seemed to get stronger and stronger instead of weaker and weaker, like he did. Old-time people were tough.

The next morning they cut grass and cooked beans.

There was a place near the cabin where tall grass grew in the summer. Yellow straw was sticking up there out of the snow. Natasha had them take the scythe from the cache and cut a big pile of dried grass.

They needed that grass to hide their traps when they were set. Grass was good for lots of other things, too. It was good for dog beds, Natasha said, and in the old days people used it to stuff inside their mukluks.

Dried grass would keep feet dry and warm. "We didn't have no knitted socks and felt liners then. Just socks we made out of rabbit skin, with the fur inside. That's *tilth*, we call it."

Sister tried to say *tilth* the way Natasha said it, with a lot of leaking air at the end. Natasha laughed, scornfully. None of these kids could speak Indian, nowadays.

"Some of those old miners, when they came into the country, didn't wear socks either. They wrapped their feet with long strips of cloth. That's so they could unwind those strips and hang them up at night over the stove, and they dried fast. Faster than knitted socks."

Toughboy looked at Natasha with interest. He had never thought about socks for a moment. He'd never thought to ask what people used for socks before there was knitting.

There was a whole world that happened before he and Sister were born, and they had missed it. They didn't even know what questions to ask to find out about it.

Toughboy wished he'd been born in those days. Things were more interesting then.

That afternoon Natasha took the number two galvanized washtub from its nail on the side of the house. She had Toughboy and Sister make three trips to the river for water because she was going to boil beans.

Natasha poured the whole twenty-pound burlap bag of beans into the tub to soak. Then she made a fire outside where she and her husband had cooked their dog food. She got the fire really blazing and then Toughboy helped her set the tub on the iron frame over the fire. Toughboy and Sister couldn't believe that she meant to cook all those beans at once.

"Papa used to do this every winter," said Natasha. "He learned it when he worked at the mining camp. Cook all the beans at once, then freeze them. When you come in at night, been walking your line all day, you just put some of them frozen beans in the skillet and some little meat you have and you got supper. Good one, too."

She boiled those beans nearly all day, and then she spooned them out in piles on the sheets of plywood that had covered the windows. When the piles of beans were frozen she took the hammer and pounded on the plywood to break the piles loose. She put those frozen chunks of beans in a burlap bag that she hung outside from the roof pole at the back of the cabin. And then the beans were done.

## ✳✳ 9 ✳✳

THAT NIGHT THEY HAD SOME OF THE beans and fried bacon cut from the big slab.

When they'd finished eating, Toughboy was too full to move. He lay on his bunk thinking about the burlap bag tied to the roof pole. He liked the idea of having supper ready in the bag, whenever they wanted it. It made him feel good, knowing that there was a lot of food in the cabin and in the cache.

They'd almost run out of food at fish camp one summer, so he worried about having enough food. Here they couldn't go hungry, that was for sure.

He leaned over the bunk to look at Natasha. "What did the Indians eat before they had beans, Natasha?"

She frowned. Sister knew that meant she didn't know the answer to the question. It made Natasha cross when they asked questions she didn't know the answers to, but they didn't know if she knew the answer or not until they asked.

"They had everything to eat," she snapped. "Lots of things we eat they ate. I don't know what it was, but they ate things we don't know about. Some roots and things we forgot about now. They had lots to eat."

Then she said, "Those were hard times the Indians had in them days. Lots of times they starved to death."

Natasha could say one thing and a completely different thing the next moment. It drove Toughboy crazy when she did that.

She opened the door of the stove and put in two pieces of spruce. "Papa told me lots of stories about starving times. In the spring, especially, when there's no snow and no birds, that's the bad time. Papa told me how they eat the inside of the willows then, that white part when you take the bark off.

"One time Papa told me about when he was

little they had to eat the rawhide on their sleds and snowshoes.

"When the stores come people like to stay around them. That's the first time we got villages, because of the stores. People know they won't starve no more with the store there. Too many hard times in those days."

Natasha closed the door to the stove and adjusted the damper.

"When I was little Mamma killed a spruce hen on the trail there in front of our camp and she cut it open and took out the guts and she said, 'You eat that.' I couldn't eat anything so awful, still warm, and I cried. She yelled at me. 'You have to learn to eat stuff like that for when the starving times come. You have to eat anything.' But Papa, he said, 'Leave her alone.' He didn't like those old ways to raise kids after he worked at the mining camps."

Natasha smiled smugly to herself. "Papa always babied me," she said. When she got that look Sister knew that she wouldn't have liked Natasha at all when she was a little girl.

"You kids eat good now. When I was a little girl there was no moose or caribou around here.

Not like there is now. They was somewhere up north. We never see them in our country. We had nothing but rabbits and spruce hens. Little things like that. And our fish.

"Sometimes when there is nothing to eat we can eat those little black fish. You can almost always find some of them in those little grass lakes."

Natasha was quiet for a long time and Toughboy and Sister were almost asleep when she suddenly said, "Mamma always froze the blood of the animals she catches. Then you could put that frozen blood in boiling water and make a soup. Blood soup."

Toughboy and Sister couldn't help making horrible faces when she said that.

She glared at them. "What you kids know about anything? You never had to be hungry. Now you're all spoiled."

They cut dry wood all the next day behind the cabin, and at the end of the day Natasha had them get two extra buckets of water and she set the buckets on the stove to heat for a bath.

She told them to bring in the number two tub

and hang it near the stove so it would get hot, too. It wouldn't do any good to heat the water if they were going to pour it into a frozen tub.

"Papa said he never had no baths while he was growing up. They'd just roll him around in the snow, bare naked. Made tough babies that way."

Toughboy was beginning to think the old-time people sat around and thought up ways to torture their children. He looked at Natasha quickly to make sure that she wasn't getting any ideas about rolling them around in the snow.

When the water was nearly boiling and the cabin windows were steamed up, Natasha put the tub behind the curtain and poured in some of the hot water. Then she mixed in cold water until it was just right. They'd take turns. They didn't throw out the water when they were finished, they just added more hot water for the next person. So the last one was the luckiest because the last one got the deepest water.

As she was going to sleep, Sister wondered what they'd do without that number two washtub. And what had the old-time people used before they had washtubs? But she was too sleepy to ask.

## ✳✳ 10 ✳✳

THE NEXT MORNING THEY GOT UP AT five. Now that their work around the cabin was finished, it was time to set the lines.

Sister put the coffee on while Natasha made a pot of oatmeal. They drank coffee and ate pilot crackers and stewed prunes, and oatmeal with canned milk and brown sugar.

They hurried to do their chores. These had to be done in the morning because they would be too tired at night. Toughboy brought in the wood while Sister ran with the buckets and the ice pick to the water hole. Natasha did the dishes and swept the dirt floor.

Natasha filled their backpacks with the things they'd need. There were number one marten traps and straw in Toughboy's pack and the bait fish and tools in Natasha's. In Sister's pack there were matches and their lunch. They each would carry a little hatchet for clearing brush out of the trail.

They had to dress very carefully to spend the whole day outdoors. Natasha watched how they put on their clothes. They'd be far away from the cabin and couldn't come in when they felt cold. They had to dress so they would stay warm.

First there was their long underwear, which they slept in. Over that their jeans and flannel shirts, and then their snow pants, which each had a bib to cover their chests. They must wear one pair of cotton socks and one pair of wool socks. Socks must never be tight or their feet would get cold right away.

Sister wanted to wear her new mukluks, but it was still too warm. Mukluks had moose-hide bottoms, so they weren't any good if the snow was wet. They had to wear their shoepacks until it was colder.

They wore short jackets over the snow pants, and knitted wool caps.

On top of all that were the long canvas over-parkas that Natasha had brought for them. These slipped over their heads and had big pockets in the front.

They would pull up the hood if the wind blew. The hoods had wolverine ruffs. Wolverine was the best kind of ruff because it didn't frost up in the cold like a wolf or a fox ruff.

They each wore a pair of cotton work gloves and over those a pair of big moose-hide mitts. The mitts were fastened to braided yarn harnesses that went around their necks, so the mitts could never be lost. There were big yarn pom-poms on the harness pieces that went across the chest and at the ends of the harnesses, at the wrists.

When you didn't need them you tied the mittens behind your back, out of the way.

The backs of Natasha's mitts were made of otter and she'd sewn a beautiful wristband with inlaid pieces of fur. She had braided a red yarn harness for her mitts, and the pom-poms were as big around as teacups.

Sister wished she had a pair of mitts like that.

They started out at seven-thirty, and the moon, still bright, lit up the whole river. They walked slowly, chopping away the willows that had overgrown the trail.

Natasha had two lines, a long one and a short one. The long one was seven miles to the end, fourteen miles altogether. That was the one they were setting today.

When they came to the bend of the river the sun began to rise and the sky flooded with pink and purple light. Blue clouds floated in that brilliant sky and birds swooped and glided far ahead of them, as if they were drunk on the colors.

The river was wide there, and far away there were hills and miles and miles of spruce trees edging the river.

Sister thought how wonderful it was to be so far away from everything. It was so quiet.

Just then an angry sound ripped the silence, and far, far above them a tiny jet began to write a white line in the morning sky.

Even if you go as far away as you can, thought Sister, there will still be something to remind you of the big world outside all these trees. Even if you went to the middle of the desert in Australia there would be something.

It could never be the way it was in the old days.

# 11

NATASHA SHOWED THEM THE PLACES on a spruce tree where a porcupine had been gnawing. Porcupines could climb trees, she said. Lots of people didn't know that. If you couldn't catch anything else, sometimes people could catch porcupines because they move so slowly. "Don't need no gun, or nothing. Just club them with a stick. Good eating, too."

If they saw a scattering of spruce needles on the snow that would tell them that there was a spruce hen up in that tree, eating.

Every so often Natasha would stop and hack away some brush and there would be one of her old marten traps. Toughboy didn't know how she knew where each one was. You couldn't see them at all as you were walking the trail. Natasha tied a bright pink surveyor's ribbon to a branch near each trap, because she said Toughboy would never be able to find the traps when she wasn't with him.

Natasha's traps were pole sets. A thin spruce pole was nailed at a slant against a tree. The trap was nailed by its chain to the place where the pole and the tree met, about four feet up the tree. The marten would run up the pole and step onto the trap.

If the old trap had broken or rusted she'd nail on one of the new traps from Toughboy's pack. She'd set the trap with a piece of the bait fish and cover it carefully with a little dried grass.

They saw a few rabbits, which still had dark patches in their fur. In a few weeks, when more snow had fallen, they would be all white. Natasha said some years the rabbits were everywhere, and in those years they would catch lots of lynx with wire snares.

She showed them how to whistle at a rabbit. If you whistle, that rabbit will stop right there and listen and you can get a good shot with your twenty-two.

Toughboy wished he'd see a rabbit so he could try the whistle. Then a big rabbit crashed through the willows right onto his path, but it was going too fast for Toughboy to even think about whistling at it. It had scared him so badly that his heart was nearly jumping out of his chest.

By the time they reached the end of the seven-mile line, Toughboy didn't think he could walk another step. He threw himself down in the snow at the side of the trail and stretched out his arms and legs. He stared at the blue sky and thought of his bunk at the cabin.

He had never walked so far before, and he felt as if he'd loosened his legs from their hip sockets. His heels hurt him and he wanted to take his boots off. And they still had to turn around and go back again.

He could tell Sister was tired, too. She stuck her tongue out like Mutt did when he had been running, to show him that she was worn out.

They looked at Natasha, who was over seventy. Maybe nearly eighty. She didn't look even a little bit tired.

Natasha told Sister to get the dry meat and pilot crackers out of her pack. "Look," she said to Toughboy. "I'll show you how to make a fire on the trail."

Toughboy wished she'd just make the fire herself and let him lie there, but he didn't say so.

She showed Toughboy the little gray branches under a tiny spruce tree. "Anywhere you have these spruce trees, underneath there's these little dry twigs. You can use that to start a fire anytime."

They each gathered a handful from the little trees by the side of the trail, and then Natasha chopped up some dead willow branches with her hatchet. She put a match to the little pile of spruce tinder and when it was flaming she added the dry wood. In no time there was a nice little fire.

She took a one-pound coffee can from Sister's pack and filled it with snow. She set the can in the fire, and when the water was boiling she added tea.

She poured the tea into the three tin mugs from Sister's pack and got out the jar of sugar, and they had the best lunch anyone could imagine, sitting right there at the end of the trail in the snow.

After drinking the tea Toughboy felt as if he could walk again. But he didn't think he'd ever be as tough as Natasha. Or the old-timers. He didn't even think he cared, he was so tired.

That night Toughboy and Sister didn't eat any dinner. After they'd hung up their clothes to dry, they lay on their bunks and were asleep in seconds. They slept so hard it felt as if they had been sleeping just minutes when Natasha woke them up the next morning.

## ✳✳ 12 ✳✳

THE NEXT DAY THEY WERE GOING TO
set the short line. Toughboy was glad they would
only be walking eight miles that day, instead of
fourteen.

When she saw how relieved he looked, Natasha
jeered, "Don't get happy. The short line goes up
two hills, so it's harder than the long line."

Toughboy couldn't imagine anything harder
than the long line. His legs were sore and stiff.
He almost groaned out loud when he sat down
to pull his wool socks on. Why didn't Natasha
get sore? Old-time people must be made tougher,
he could see that.

Natasha said you had to check your traps every
other day. If you left the fur in the trap for longer

than a day the shrews might chew on it and ruin the skin. Only lazy trappers let their fur get ruined.

They would walk the short line one day, and the long line the next.

Natasha said that three people were better than two and two were better than one, because it was very hard for just one person to trap. There was too much for one person to do.

There was so much work every day, Sister didn't see how they would ever have done their schoolwork if they'd brought it. And she would not have had time to read those books, either.

The old-time people didn't have time to go to school very much. And when they were out of school they didn't have time to do anything but work, work, work all their lives. Working to stay warm, and working to stay fed.

And when they'd used up all their time doing both of those things, there wasn't any time left to do anything else. Sister liked to work, but she wanted time to do something besides that. She didn't know what, exactly, but she'd know some-day.

*  *  *

As they walked along the short line Natasha would stop at the grass lakes and sloughs and creeks to teach them about the ice.

Grass lakes were shallow ponds full of marsh grass, and so the water froze differently there than the water in creeks. Sloughs were branches of the river and their ice was different from the ice on the river or the creeks or the grass lakes.

Every day the ice would change with the weather. You had to know what you were looking at and what the sounds of the ice meant.

You had to know where the swift places in the river were, because the ice would always be dangerous there.

You must test the ice with a stick or your ice pick, and listen for the dull sound of sturdy ice.

There might be an open place in the river and a thin layer of ice would form over that water. Then it would snow on top of that and you would think there was thick ice under that snow. Lots of people drowned that way. You had to learn to read the signs on the snow cover, and to be careful.

After it had snowed and you couldn't see the ice anymore, you had to be careful of overflow. That was the most dangerous thing of all. Water would ooze out of cracks in the ice when there was a heavy snow or if it got very cold or very warm all of a sudden. The slush would lie under the snow and you couldn't see it.

Sometimes snow machines or airplanes would get stuck in the overflow. They would freeze into that slush right away, and it would take a lot of work to get them out again. That's why Billy had dragged his skis on the ice before he landed.

If you stepped in overflow you'd get your boots wet and then your feet might freeze. Natasha said if their boots got wet through, they must stop and make a fire right away and take off their shoepacks or mukluks and socks and get them dry before they went on. She knew a lot of people who had frozen their feet trying to get home first. If your feet were badly frozen they might have to be cut off in the hospital.

"Why don't we always carry extra socks and mukluks in our packs?" asked Sister. "Then we'd always be safe, and we wouldn't even have to make a fire."

Natasha looked disgusted. "You don't get ready for a bad thing to happen. You just make it happen that way. That will give you bad luck."

That seemed very silly to Sister.

They were on the ridge near the end of the short trail when a huge owl flew along ahead of them as if it were guiding them. Its wings nearly touched the trees on both sides of the trail, it was so big. It glided and swooped ahead of them for nearly a mile, silent.

Natasha finally stopped on the trail and talked to it in Indian. Then it flew off the trail and left them, as if she'd told it to go away.

Owls could speak in Indian, but when they did they would tell you something bad. Maybe somebody would be going to die or an accident was going to happen. This owl didn't say anything, but still it had made Natasha nervous, the way it just flew along ahead of them. Owls knew too much.

Ravens were different. When ravens flew above them their wings were noisy, beating the sky like laundry flapping in the wind.

Toughboy and Sister loved to listen to the

ravens. They had so many voices, you could never tell which one they would use. Sometimes they cried *bonk, bonk,* like hollow drums, and sometimes they screeched in a horrible way that made Toughboy and Sister laugh.

Natasha said when you were out hunting, the ravens would make a certain sound to tell you if there was a moose or caribou nearby. They would help you out if they felt like it. Toughboy and Sister thought that ravens weren't serious enough to give much good advice.

# ✷✷ 13 ✷✷

EVERY NIGHT, AS SOON AS THEY CAME into the cabin, they had to take care of their clothes. No matter how tired they were. That was the most important thing to learn at the trapline. If you didn't take care of your clothes the right way you might freeze your feet or hands.

First you had to put your boots by the fire to dry. You took out the felt liners and hung them and your wool socks on the clothesline over the stove with clothespins. Socks and liners had to be perfectly dry when you put them into your boots in the morning. You could freeze your feet if they were damp.

Then you had to take the gloves out of your moose-hide mittens and hang both the mittens and gloves up there over the heat. Your snow pants and your parka and your over-parka and your scarf and your hat all had to be hung up, too.

Toughboy and Sister had to stand on a stool to do this, and it seemed to take forever. Toughboy was always half-disgusted by the time he was through. But in the morning when he got dressed again, it was a good feeling to put on all those warm dry clothes.

Over the stove and behind the stove the lines were always full of drying clothes. Sister hated that because they made the cabin look untidy. As soon as the things were dry she'd hang them back on their nails by the door.

They listened to the radio every morning while they ate breakfast and every night while they washed the dishes, so they could hear the messages. If people in Fairbanks wanted to send news to someone in the villages or on the traplines or at fish camp they would call the radio station and the announcer would read that message on the air.

Natasha never missed the messages.

"To the Petersons at Shaw Creek. John was sentenced to three years, one year suspended."

"Hmph," snorted Natasha. "Bad people. Always have one of their kids in jail."

"To Nick and the kids at Old Fort. Tried to get back on the mail plane today, but couldn't make it. Will be home tomorrow, weather permitting. Love from Mom."

"Kyuh," said Natasha, with contempt. "She's not fooling no one. She's in town drinking. They're not going to see her for a week, till she spent all their money. She's no good, that woman."

Sure enough, for the next few days the messages from Mom gave one excuse after another, and then there were no more. Sister wondered if the mother had ever gone home to her children.

After the dishes were washed and the messages were over, Natasha told them stories. In the old days people told stories every night in the winter.

When the stories were finished, you were supposed to say in Indian, "Now I've chewed off part of the winter."

Toughboy liked the stories about the wars between the Indians the best. Natasha told them

71

the story of the last war they had when her father was a baby.

"The Koyukuk Indians snuck down to Nulato and they chopped holes in the top of the underground houses and stuck burning canoes in the holes. When those people in there came out to get away from the smoke they shot them all with arrows."

She smiled. "Served them right. I still don't trust them Nulato people."

When Sister went to bed at night she always had to kick her feet furiously for a while to warm up her sleeping bag. But Toughboy was in the top bunk and it was always too hot up there.

One night Toughboy slept on the floor because it was so hot in the top bunk.

He felt something tugging at his hair in the middle of the night and he shook it out of his hair with a yell. His hands were shaking so, he could hardly light the lamp. In the corner where he'd flung it was a little sharp-nosed shrew, dead.

He'd wakened sister and Natasha, and they sat up to look at the shrew. Natasha said that the shrew was taking pieces of Toughboy's hair to make a nest. Toughboy could feel the short place in his hair where the shrew had bitten it off.

After that he slept in his bunk. Natasha said it wouldn't do any good to be way up there, because shrews could climb up nearly anything. So the next morning Toughboy flattened four tin cans and put them all around the legs of the bunk. He'd like to see a shrew climb up tin.

Sister had dreams that week about a huge shrew cutting her hair with a big pair of scissors.

# ✳✳ 14 ✳✳

ONE MORNING WHEN SISTER WOKE UP she could see her breath in the room. There was frost lining the door and thick frost had climbed up the windows. The fire was almost out and the room was cold, cold.

Sister wished she could stay in her sleeping bag forever. After she dressed she pulled on her parka and boots. When she lit the kerosene lamp on the table the chimney frosted up from the cold.

Then she fixed the fire. Natasha had taught her just how to do it, because at the trapline the youngest was always supposed to be the first one up. The youngest had to make the fire and get the coffee or tea ready. Sister didn't mind. She liked to make the fire. She liked to be the first one up.

She twisted the damper on the stovepipe until the handle stood straight up and down, and then she opened the sliding damper in the big square stove door. That was to let more air into the stove and to keep it from smoking. She tapped on the stovepipe with the stove poker so the chunks of soot would fall down into the stove.

She squeaked open the stove door, and with the poker scraped the red coals from the back to the front. She laid kindling on top of those coals, and the smallest pieces of split spruce on top of that.

In just a few minutes the spruce was crackling and popping. That was a warm sound and the cold didn't seem so mean anymore.

Sister went to the window to see what the temperature was. The thermometer was outside, nailed to the wall. She had to scrape away the frost to see it. She held the lamp up to the window.

Twenty below. Well, it was winter at last. Cold enough to wear her new mukluks.

Toughboy didn't have new ones this year because last year's still fit him. It made him mad that Sister was growing and he wasn't.

Sister's mukluks were made of canvas, with moose-hide bottoms, and along the top there was a pink band of embroidered trim bought from the store. There were bright pink pom-poms at the end of the braided yarn ties. Sister could hardly wait to wear them.

The clanging of the stove door woke Toughboy. He dug deeper into his sleeping bag. Someday he would be grown up and he'd never get up if he didn't want to. He wondered if you could sleep for a week if no one woke you up. He was sure he could.

In just a minute Natasha was going to tell him to get up. He'd like to be the one to tell her to get up. Maybe he should get up first, before she told him. That would show her.

He unzipped his sleeping bag and swung his legs over the edge of his bunk. As soon as he hit the floor he realized how cold it was in the room. Up in his bunk it was a lot warmer.

Sister looked at him in surprise. He never got up before Natasha.

"It's cold," she whispered. "Twenty below."

Toughboy huddled next to the stove and pulled his jeans and flannel shirt on over his long underwear. He hated it when his back was cold and his front was too hot. He put on his shoepacks and parka and gloves and went out into the dark morning to get a few bucketfuls of snow to melt in the big pot on the stove. That was for washing dishes. It was so cold out that the snow didn't have much water in it, and he had to bring in more snow than he usually did. He'd go to the water hole later.

Natasha sat up in bed when Sister brought her a cup of tea. Her gray hair fell over her shoulder in one long braid. "*Adzoo*," she said. "Cold."

Toughboy came in with the extra bucket of snow, and the cold air boiled into the cabin in angry swirls. "Shut the door quick," snapped Natasha.

The night before, Natasha had set out a bowl of sourdough to rise, so Toughboy knew there would be hotcakes for breakfast.

Sourdough hotcakes were Toughboy's favorite food in the world and he could eat at least ten if there was lots of syrup. You made syrup with a bottle of maple flavoring and sugar and water, and you boiled it for a while until it was just thick enough but not too thick. Natasha never made enough syrup, Toughboy thought.

There were always some hotcakes left over to feed to the birds. The camp robbers were big birds, fat and gray, and they weren't afraid of much. If there was nothing on the feeding shelf they would peer in the window and squawk as if demanding to be fed. Toughboy and Sister could get them to eat out of their hands if they stayed still enough.

"You'd better stay home today and cut some more spruce," Natasha told Toughboy while they were eating. "Sister and I will walk the long line. If it stays cold we might run out of wood."

Toughboy didn't like to be left by himself.

"I could cut wood when we get back," he said.

She gave him an are-you-crazy look. "It's dark then, what's the matter with you? You can't cut wood in the dark."

He thought it was pretty funny that she was so darn sure there were woodsmen who steal children, but she was going to leave him here alone anyway. He wanted to ask her if she wasn't worried that he might be carried off, but somehow it didn't seem like a good thing to do.

# ✳✳ 15 ✳✳

THEY WERE THE MOST WONDERFUL mukluks ever. Sister's feet felt as light as if she were barefoot. She ran along the trail for a while, for the sheer joy of it, the snow crunching and squeaking under her feet.

It was perfect weather for walking. Cold enough so you wouldn't get hot and sweaty in all your clothes, and the trail was just right, not soft or crumbly, but crisp and easy walking. Sister thought she could walk a hundred miles and never get tired in her new mukluks.

When the sun came up the sky was a hard bright blue, and new, heavy frost lay thick on every twig and branch. The woods looked like a sugar forest in a fairy tale.

Sister thought that winter was a lady with long white-silver hair and pale white skin and blue eyes. Blue-eyed winter, she thought.

The colder it got, the more beautiful it got. The more beautiful everything was, though, the more dangerous it was. It shouldn't be that way, thought Sister. Beautiful things should be good and bad things should be ugly. That way you couldn't get mixed up.

Natasha showed Sister the big beaver house at the slough. There was a smaller pile of sticks about twenty feet away from the house.

"That's their feed pile. They stack all their food right there, so it's ready for winter. Next time I'll bring a beaver snare to set here. That's the best food there is, beaver. Nice and fat."

Sister remembered how Mamma cooked beaver tail with her beans sometimes. All the little bones and joints in the tail would come apart and Mamma would take them out so that Toughboy wouldn't choke on them. Girls couldn't eat beaver. She asked Natasha why not.

Natasha looked down at her.

"If you eat those beavers, you'll have a hard

time when you're having your babies. That's *hutlanee*."

Sister walked behind Natasha, enjoying the way her mukluks sounded on the snow. She thought about all the things women couldn't eat in the old-time way.

She ran a little to catch up with Natasha again. "Natasha, how come it's always women who can't eat these things?"

Natasha seemed not to hear and kept walking. But finally she said, "Women were not supposed to eat too much. If you eat too much you'll take away your husband's luck. When we were young, girls had to eat a cupful of rotten grease. That's so you never eat too much."

She stopped a moment in the trail to squint at the mountains far away. It was clear, so they could see the highest mountain, Denali, there on the edge of the world.

Sister looked up into Natasha's stern face.

"In those days women were a bad-luck thing." Natasha stopped and chopped viciously at a willow with her ax.

"A woman could never touch a man's tools, or walk over his clothes, or even walk in front of him. That's *hutlanee*." Natasha threw the willows off the trail with a grunt.

"And when a girl was getting to be a woman, they would just make a place for her in the corner of the house, with a blanket hung up across it, so they couldn't see her. They call that going behind the blanket.

"When it was time for me to go behind the blanket Papa said no. He didn't like those old ways. I was just happy Papa said no, but Mamma was mad about that. She was scared when you did things wrong."

Natasha started off down the trail again and Sister crunched along behind her. How hard it must have been to live then. Hardest for the women, she thought.

Sometimes Natasha wanted the old days back. And sometimes she talked about them bitterly.

Sister wondered if you could like something and not like something at the same time.

After they'd gone another mile Natasha sat down on a fallen tree next to the trail and pulled her cigarettes and matches from her inside pocket. She lit a cigarette quickly and put her gloves back on. She pointed out to Sister a little naked tamarack tree. "That's *taat'aghalt*," she said. "That kind lose their needles in the fall, not like spruce." Sister tried the word a few times, but it didn't sound the way Natasha said it. She was glad Natasha didn't seem to notice.

Natasha smoked quietly for a while. Finally she said, "Father Jette was a priest at Nulato. A long time. He got to be an old man there. He could talk Indian, better than any other white man. He wrote down all the high words. He could talk in high Indian. Not like me. I only learned camp Indian, what we talk all the time. Nobody knows the high words anymore. But Father Jette wrote those words down so they're somewhere."

Natasha threw her cigarette butt into the snow and sat with her hands resting on her knees. Then she said, "I'd like to hear those high words again, the way those old men used to talk at potlatch when they gave speeches. Never hear it again."

Sister felt a lump in her throat. She'd never thought of words being lost. How could words be lost? She looked carefully at Natasha. Lost words, lost songs, and all the old-time ways lost. Would she and Toughboy someday have lost words? Would the ways they had now be old-time ways?

# ✴✴ 16 ✴✴

AT THE NEXT TRAP A CAMP ROBBER had been caught and was frozen in the trap. Natasha gave a snort of disgust. She snapped the trap and threw the stiff camp robber away.

Sister squatted down to look at the dead bird where it had fallen in the snow. Its bright eyes were closed. Was it one of the tame ones? Was it one that came to the feeding shelf every day, acting sassy and bossy? Oh, why had it walked on the trap?

She wished she could make it come alive.

Natasha baited the trap again with fish from her pack, and they walked on.

At the next trap there was a marten, their first. He was dead, his paw caught when he'd tried to reach the bait. Natasha took him out of the trap and ruffled his orange fur. "Good coat for so early."

Sister's heart squeezed tight in her chest. The marten's face was sweet and gentle, like a kitten, or like the animals in her first-grade reading book.

"Does it hurt, Natasha?"

"Does what hurt? What you're talking about?"

"The trap. Does it hurt when they're caught?"

She scoffed at Sister. "No. They don't have feelings like us. They let us catch them. They let us have their fur."

Natasha stuffed the dead marten in her pack, head first. The tail was hanging out. She gestured to Sister to come along.

"Sometimes they chew their own foot off to get out of the trap. Sometimes you come along and you just find a foot in the trap. Or sometimes you catch a marten with one foot gone, you know he been caught before."

Sister stood still. She could see that sweet-faced marten eating off its own foot.

She hated trapping. Tears formed in her eyes and froze on her eyelids.

She ran to get ahead of Natasha so she wouldn't have to look at that sad tail. But then she was afraid that they'd find another marten, dead or dying, at every pink ribbon by the trail.

So she walked behind, her eyes on her mukluks.

But they caught no more that day.

Long before they got home it was dark. As they came around the bend of the river they could see the cabin.

Toughboy had the lamps lit. A patch of golden light from the window lay on the snow and red sparks tumbled out of the chimney. It was a lovely sight when you were tired and cold and hungry.

They could hear music.

Toughboy was playing the radio very loudly. "Me and Bobby McGee." Sister loved that song.

There was a bright red spot on one of Toughboy's cheeks. He'd frozen it because he hadn't pulled his hood up, and it was still stinging. Natasha shook her head with disgust when she saw it.

She told Toughboy to take the marten out of

her pack and leave it on the woodpile outside. They would skin and stretch it tomorrow. "When you catch something you can't never bring it in the house the same day. That's *hutlanee*," she said.

Natasha poured water from the teakettle into the washbasin and washed her hands. When she bent to refill the teakettle with the water under the table she saw the pail was empty. She shot a furious glance at Toughboy.

"I forgot," he mumbled. He'd worked so hard cutting wood all day, and she didn't even notice what he did do. Just what he didn't do. "I'll go get it," he said.

"Eat first," said Natasha.

Sister and Toughboy brought their plates of beans close to the stove to eat. There was frost on the walls, and only the middle of the cabin, near the stove, seemed warm. Natasha laughed at them.

"What you going to do if you live in a tent? You kids are spoiled."

She hung her mukluks over the stove and carefully spread her over-parka over the back of the chair so it would dry.

"Mary Potter had her first baby in a tent that

winter that was so cold. They put it between them to sleep, but when they woke up in the morning it was dead. Froze."

When Natasha told those stories Toughboy and Sister felt cold, even though they weren't. They looked at the frosty door hinges, and the ice on the windows.

They wished they were back in the village.

# 17

AFTER DINNER TOUGHBOY PUT HIS WIN-
ter gear back on, took the bucket, and went to
the water hole.

Sister took the washbasin and carried it outside. As she threw the dirty wash-water into the
snow she saw that Toughboy had forgotten to
take the ice pick. He'd get all the way to the
water hole and have to come back. She'd put her
things on and take it to him.

Toughboy didn't remember about the ice pick
until he got to the water hole. He was tired and
cross and angry at himself, so he threw the water
bucket down hard, and started back toward the
cabin. Across the river he could see Sister coming
toward him. It was very dark, but he could see

the light of her flashlight. It was jiggling up and down, so she must be running.

Sister cut across the slough, running fast, taking a shortcut to the water hole. She was singing that Bobby McGee song in her head, trying to remember the words in the chorus, when she heard the ice pop under her feet. She stopped so fast she nearly fell over on her face.

She knew when you heard that sound you shouldn't go any further without testing the ice. She gave the ice ahead of her a hard jab with he ice pick.

There was a sharp crack, and a whole piece of ice under her feet tipped into the water.

As soon as she felt herself sinking she fought and kicked her feet so that her head wouldn't go under the water. She grabbed the edge of the ice and held on, still kicking.

The edge snapped off under her mitten, and she began to sink backward. She kicked frantically and grabbed the edge of the ice again. But it snapped off.

She threw one arm up on the ice, reaching as far as she could. Then she threw her other arm up. The ice held, and she clung there for a minute, panting. Under the ice she could see the glow of her flashlight. She wondered if it had reached the bottom of the slough yet.

Slowly she pulled one knee up onto the ice.

She held her breath but the ice broke off under her knee and her leg plunged back into the water. Her legs were so numb that she didn't think she could pull them up again.

Her wet moose-hide mitts had frozen to the top of the ice now. She pulled her hands out of the mitts and held on to the harnesses. Slowly, slowly she pulled herself out of the water, holding onto the harnesses.

The mittens were frozen tight, and held her until she was all the way out of the water.

She was on top of the ice now, and was slowly creeping forward toward the bank.

There was another loud crack and the whole sheet of ice she was on snapped off.

The icy water splashed in her face, and again she fought to keep her head from going under the water.

Suddenly a hand reached out and grabbed her parka hood. She knew without looking that it was Toughboy. He dragged Sister up on the ice.

Then, on his knees, he slowly inched his way back, backward, until his feet touched the bank. He pulled her by the hood and half dragged her up the bank.

"Walk!" he yelled at her.

She couldn't feel her feet so she wasn't sure she was walking.

Sister thought of a movie she'd seen at the community hall. It was about the desert. A cowboy had crawled through the desert, dying of the heat, the sun was glaring down on him, the cruel hot sun. She imagined that she was crawling through the desert. Suddenly, she remembered the words that she'd forgotten in the song. She stopped to sing them in her head.

Toughboy pulled her roughly. "Come on! Keep walking. It's only a little more!"

Sister didn't answer and he didn't know what to do. She seemed frozen where she stood. He picked her up and staggered a few steps with her. She was too heavy for him. He put her down again and threw her over his shoulder the way he'd seen men carry fifty-pound sacks of flour or dog feed.

When he pushed open the cabin door and set

her in the middle of the floor, she was covered in chunks of ice from her waist down. Natasha stared for a moment and then got up quickly and shut the door. "Get her clothes off her," was all she said.

All of Sister's insides felt hard and cold, like ice that had to melt very slowly. She was afraid she'd never get warm again. When Natasha asked her what had happened Sister shook her head and wouldn't speak. Being in the water was so horrible that she wouldn't think of it again. Maybe she'd never get warm if she let herself remember it.

When they'd rolled Sister into her sleeping bag she went to sleep immediately, and dreamed all night of the lost flashlight.

## ✳✳ 18 ✳✳

IT WAS COLD FOR TWO BRIGHT DAYS, and the place where Sister had fallen into the slough was covered with ice in one day. Then the sky grew soft and gray as pussy willows, and it snowed.

It snowed without stopping for two days, and you couldn't see the place where Sister had fallen through at all. They must never again leave the trail, Natasha warned them. You knew the trail was safe. Look what had happened to Sister when she took a shortcut.

The feeding shelf was crowded with birds because their regular food was covered with snow.

Snow was slumped in deep soft drifts on all the branches. The slightest wind would knock it down.

Mutt slept outdoors when the cabin was too hot for him, curled in a circle, his tail covering his eyes and nose. The snow drifted softly around him while he slept, dreaming wolf dreams, Sister thought.

It was soft heavy snow with lots of water in it, so they stayed home for those two snowing days and melted a lot of snow to wash their clothes and take baths.

"Papa wore the same underwear all winter," Natasha told them. "Never washed it."

When Toughboy and Sister looked shocked she laughed.

"Not this kind of underwear. Indian kind. They used to take strips of rabbit skin and weave it into underwear. It was just warm. By summertime the fur was all worn off, so you could wear it in the summer too. Good for all year."

Toughboy wondered what it felt like to wear fur next to your bare skin. Especially rabbit fur. It was so soft and shed so easily. He thought of rabbit hairs sticking all over your skin when you got sweaty. He was glad for his cotton long johns.

They washed so many things the wet clothes wouldn't all fit on the lines over the stove, so they hung them outside to dry. When Sister carried in the clothes they were frozen stiff. She stacked them on the woodpile next to the stove to thaw. When they thawed they were a little damp again, so they had to be hung over the stove for a while.

The clean clothes smelled delicious. They smelled like new snow, the best smell in the world.

Toughboy put on snowshoes to walk the trail to the outhouse. He walked back and forth until the trail was packed down.

Natasha brought a frozen marten into the house and thawed it. Then she showed them just how it was to be skinned. She wouldn't let them skin marten yet themselves. The skins were too valuable and they'd ruin them until they knew what they were doing. They'd get some little minks or weasels soon, and they could practice on those. Toughboy watched very carefully, sure he'd never be able to remember everything.

Natasha had a thin little knife that she used only for skinning. First she slit the legs, and then the tail, and then she carefully pulled the skin up over the marten's carcass until it reached the ears.

Then she began to cut carefully around the eyes and snout.

Sister turned away. She didn't want to learn to skin. She hated it that they'd killed that lovely soft thing.

Why was the world made so that you must always be killing?

All around their cabin in the new snow were little looping chains, interlocking rings making lovely patterns in the snow. Those were ptarmigan tracks.

When Toughboy and Sister went to get water, the soft snowbank suddenly exploded in front of them and a dozen ptarmigan went flying in every direction.

They had been sleeping under the snow. They scared Toughboy and Sister so badly they had to sit down and wait until their knees stopped shaking and their breath wasn't ragged.

The fat ptarmigan sat up in the trees and looked down at them, pure white and velvety. Only when they flew could you see the black velvet fan on their tails.

Sister thought they were the most beautiful birds in the world.

Next to the ptarmigan tracks Sister liked the tiny tracks of the shrews the best. The shrews lived under the snow and had little towns and trails and a whole life down there.

Once in a while Mutt would stop and look down at the snow and cock his head this way and that, listening to a sound Toughboy and Sister couldn't hear. And then suddenly he'd start to dig frantically, making the snow fly between his legs. But he never found what he was looking for.

Sister tried to imagine what the world sounded like to Mutt. He could hear things they couldn't hear. And could smell things they couldn't smell.

When Mutt was out in the woods he dashed about, busy with his nose, rushing here and there, distracted by another thing before he'd finished exploring the first thing. Maybe the woods seemed noisy and crowded and busy to Mutt, when they seemed so quiet and calm to them.

## ✳✳ 19 ✳✳

THE SKY CLEARED AND IT GOT COLDER.
It was time to check their traps again.

They had to brush the snow away from every
trap, and they had to pack the trail down again.
It would be a hard day. Toughboy and Natasha
would check the short line first, so Toughboy
could get used to walking on snowshoes. Natasha
was keeping Sister home for a few more days to
be sure she wouldn't get sick from falling through
the ice.

The trail was badly drifted. It was very slow
walking.

Natasha was always way ahead of Toughboy.
He could never walk the way she did on snowshoes. It looked like regular walking, not clumsy

and ducklike, the way Toughboy and Sister walked on their snowshoes. Maybe the old-time people were built differently.

Toughboy's lips were cracked and red from the cold where he'd wet his lips with his tongue. There was a black spot on his cheek where he'd frozen it, and it was stinging with cold. It would be easy to freeze that place again so he kept pulling his hand out of his mitten to warm it.

They saw dozens of fresh animal tracks in the deep, clean snow.

Lynx tracks were round circles dented in the snow, and rabbit tracks were long and fast-looking. Sometimes there would be a place where the rabbit's tail had rested.

On their way back home Natasha and Toughboy came upon a place where two moose had come out of the woods and were walking on their trail. Their tracks were deep troughs, as deep as Toughboy's knee.

It was a cow and calf, Natasha said.

She stopped where the moose tracks started and made a fire for tea.

Toughboy sat down and, with his fingers, tried to scoop out the snow packed into the tops of his shoepacks. But there was so much he had to take his boots off and shake the snow out.

Natasha had the fire blazing now. Toughboy filled the coffee can with snow and set it on the fire. You had to put it on just right or it would tip over and put out the fire, and then you'd have to start all over.

Natasha looked with disgust at the deep moose tracks on the trail.

"Look at our trail, all them big holes punched in it. Makes me want to spit," she said.

Life was easy in the woods if the trail was good, but not so easy if it wasn't. And there wasn't anything you could do about it. You just had to take it as it comes and be ready for it.

At the grass lake they could see yellow places in the snow where the water had seeped up through the cracks. There was overflow everywhere after a big snow.

When they got back to the cabin the full moon was shining down on them. The moonlight and the new snow made it almost as bright as day.

Wolves were howling across the river. A lovely sound, like moonlight, cool and painful. Natasha stopped on the top of the bank with Toughboy to listen.

"Natasha, would you like to go to the moon?" he asked suddenly.

"Kyuh." She made her disgusted sound. "You couldn't go to the moon." He looked at her quickly to see if she meant that.

"You could," he said indignantly. "There were people on the moon already. When I was in fourth grade they did that."

"That's just lies they're telling you," snorted Natasha. "That's *hutlanee*, to talk that way." And she walked down the bank and into the willows.

Toughboy stared after her for a minute. There were lots of things Natasha knew. But there were some things she didn't know.

# 20

AFTER A WEEK OR SO, NATASHA SPRANG the traps on the long line. It was dead country, she said. That meant that there were no signs of marten there.

She didn't spring the traps on the first mile of the long line because that part went through the trees, where there were plenty of marten.

The short line was good country because it was in the trees.

So they didn't walk the long line anymore. Toughboy was glad because they could check the short line during daylight. They didn't have to start before sunrise and stay out so late.

* * *

A few weeks later Sister was staying home while Toughboy and Natasha checked traps. She was going to bake bread for the week.

She was happy for any excuse to stay home. She didn't want to help trap anymore.

There were five marten skins drying on their stretcher boards. Sister tried not to look at them, the empty spaces where their eyes had been. But she couldn't get away from the musky smell of the marten. It got into her clothes and hair and teeth.

She wondered if Mamma had felt sorry for the animals Daddy killed. She was pretty sure she hadn't.

She didn't know why she always thought differently from anyone she knew. Even Mamma and Daddy.

She liked to stay behind by herself, and do the dishes, and clean the cabin. It made her happy when everything was tidy.

She'd wash out all the dish towels and hang them over the fire until they were dry, and she'd scrub the table hard with the brush. She'd sweep the dirt floor and pile up wood next to the stove.

It was like playing house. She pretended that

she had lots of very clean children and a husband who was outside working. She was trying to decide what the children's names should be. She had all the first names and all of the middle names except one. It was the middle names that were hardest.

She was thinking so hard about that name that she jumped when Mutt gave a sudden sharp bark. When her heart slowed down she realized that it was his friendly bark, not his warning bark.

Sister opened the door to see what Mutt was barking at. She saw a bull moose on the trail by the tall spruces, eating the bark on the willows.

His rough coat was dark brown, but he looked almost red in the pink sunrise. He was graceful, raising his huge head and flattening his ears to reach some branches over his head. He paid no attention to Mutt's barking and went on eating slowly, calmly.

His antlers scraped against the willow trunk as he munched. The horns made a dry, hollow sound, like wild rhubarb stalks in the fall wind. Soon he would lose those horns, and someone would find them lying in the woods.

Sister watched, entranced. His brown eyes

were kind. She'd never seen a moose so close before. He was magic, like the unicorns in stories. So beautiful and strong.

She could get up on his back and ride away into the woods with him, and he'd take her to wonderful places.

She watched him, almost without breathing, until he melted away into the tall spruces and was gone.

# 21

A WEEK LATER, JUST AFTER DAYBREAK, Mutt began to bark again. This time it was his danger bark. He didn't like what was coming.

In a few minutes they heard jangling bells, just like the ones in movies on Santa Claus's sled. And coming down the trail was a dog team.

There were only three dogs, but they were bigger than any dogs Toughboy and Sister had ever seen, and in front of them trotted a merry little black-and-white dog with a red collar.

The bells were sewed to the harnesses of the big dogs. They were hitched to a heavy sled, made of lumber.

Riding the back runners was a tall thin man

in a canvas over-parka, his beard and mustache and eyebrows and eyelashes and ruff all frosted and covered with icicles.

Toughboy and Sister looked quickly at Natasha for an explanation. "Nelson," she said.

She wasn't surprised, that was sure. Mutt was barking furiously at the little dog, so Toughboy grabbed him by the collar.

"Quiet, Mutt!"

Natasha stood outside watching as the man pulled the sled up in front of the cabin and pushed his frosted hood back. He pulled one of his hands out of his heavy mitts and ran his bare hand slowly over his mustache to thaw the ice as he looked approvingly at his dogs, stretched in a smart row. He picked a few stubborn pieces of ice from his beard and mustache, and only then did he look at Natasha.

He nodded, in what was neither a friendly nor an unfriendly way. Natasha nodded back in the same way. Sister was sure that they had known each other for a long time, and had nodded this way many times before.

Nelson threw his mitts in the sled and pulled

his over-parka over his head. When he emerged they could see that he was quite old. Maybe as old as Natasha. The hair on his head was skimpy and white with a lot of pink scalp showing through. He followed Natasha into the cabin without looking at Toughboy and Sister.

Natasha pulled the kettle from the back of the wood stove to the front so it would come to a boil, and gestured with her head at the teapot to show Sister to get it ready.

"Do you want me to tie up your dogs?" Toughboy asked.

"No, son. Those dogs don't need tying. They just sit and wait for me. They're not going no place without me," he said, laughing.

"How far did you come?" asked Toughboy. He was too curious to worry about being rude. "What kind of dogs are those? Did that little one run with you all along?"

The man laughed again and Natasha grunted. "Kids nowadays don't know nothing about dogs," she said.

Nelson smiled at Toughboy. "Them are Mackenzie huskies. Old-time dogs. Better than these little sled dogs they got nowadays."

"And what does that little dog do?" asked Sister.

"Well, that's what you call a loose leader. That's a bossy little dog. That's Charlie. He tells them big dogs to slow down or speed up or turn this way or that, and if they don't do what he says, Charlie'll come back and nip them till they go the right way."

Sister and Toughboy smiled at the idea of that little dog bossing those big dogs around. They'd like to see that.

Nelson worked a small mining claim in the summers over the hill from Natasha's trapline cabin. It was only about fifteen miles away, but it was fifteen miles of hard trail, up and down through thick brush.

He had been in the country since the early days, when the hills were full of miners. Natasha said he was the last old prospector left.

He went over the hills to McGrath every spring to get his food and supplies for the coming year, so he hadn't been to their village for almost twenty years. But he talked about his last visit there as if it were yesterday.

Nelson had a crazy smile. The corners of his mouth nearly touched his ears when he smiled all out. Other times he only smiled with one half of his mouth. Toughboy and Sister got so interested in watching his face move they sometimes forgot to pay attention to his words.

Every year Nelson used to visit Natasha at winter camp, once before the hard part of winter started, and once in the spring when there was a hard crust on the snow and it was easy to travel cross-country.

He had heard from Billy Cross that Natasha was in the country this winter, and he'd come as soon as he'd gotten ready for the bad weather. A good time to visit, he said, before the bad cold set in.

All that afternoon he kept them laughing with his old mining camp stories and his funny smile. Then he suddenly looked sad and said, "Well, them days are gone and they'll never come no more."

Sister thought he sounded like Natasha. The

old days he loved were different from Natasha's old days, but they were both very sorry to have them gone.

Were all old people homesick for the way things used to be?

## ✳✳ 22 ✳✳

NELSON WAS GETTING READY TO MAKE the trip back home a few hours later when they heard his little dog barking furiously, his voice high-pitched and desperate.

They all ran outside, and there was Sister's moose at the willow trees again. The little dog was snapping furiously at the moose's heels.

Nelson yelled and swore angrily at his dog, but Charlie paid no attention. He leaped up and nipped at the moose's hindquarters, and Tough-boy and Sister both saw that the moose's ears were laid back and the hair on his hump was standing straight up.

Those gentle brown eyes were flashing white now. The moose lowered his head and tossed his horns at the dog. He stamped his feet and a long shiver rippled all down his huge muscular body.

Nelson ran up the trail to pull Charlie away.

The moose swung one foreleg at Charlie and Charlie darted out of range, barking savagely, his teeth bared in an ugly grimace.

Suddenly Charlie lost his courage and began to run away from the moose with his tail between his legs. The moose started after him.

When Nelson saw his dog and the moose racing toward him, he turned around and began to run, too. When the moose caught up with him, Nelson dived off the trail into the snow.

The moose stopped and turned back toward Nelson, his head down to scoop Nelson up on his horns. It happened so quickly that no one could think of anything to do.

Sister ran toward them as fast as she could, hollering. The moose moved back a step when he saw her and rolled his eyes. She stopped in front of him and clapped her hands together the way a teacher claps at a noisy class. "Shoo," she screamed, and clapped at him again.

She had no idea that he'd look so big close up. She only came up to his nose.

The moose threw his head up in the air and trotted off in an insulted way back to the willow thicket, and disappeared into the woods.

Charlie was hiding under the cache, but as soon as the moose was gone he began to bark wildly again.

Toughboy and Sister and Natasha waded into the deep snow to help Nelson up.

He was hurt. The moose's horns had raked him as he dove into the snow, and he'd been kicked with those dangerous hooves.

At first he didn't look as if he was conscious, but then he opened his eyes and struggled to his feet when they held him by the arms. His breath was knocked out of him and he couldn't answer their questions. He walked slowly down the trail toward the cabin, supported on either side by Toughboy and Natasha.

When they got Nelson back to the cabin, Natasha told Toughboy and Sister to get their jackets on and wait outside while she examined the old man. They sat on the chopping block and talked excitedly about what had just happened. Natasha came to the door about fifteen minutes later and threw the wash water out of the basin.

Then she took one of the marten stretchers from the woodpile and chopped a piece off with one blow of the ax. She jerked her head to show they could come back in.

The old man was lying in Natasha's bed, dressed in Natasha's clean flannel nightgown. His eyes were closed and he looked as if he'd fallen asleep. Then he suddenly opened his eyes and grinned at Sister. "Well, girlie," he said, "looks like you rescued me. That old moose was going to toss me from here to Texas if you didn't change his mind for him."

Toughboy wished it had been him. He wouldn't have clapped his hands in that silly way, of course. He would have grabbed a big stick, and roaring a terrible roar he would have fought the moose off with one hand while he picked up Nelson with the other.

"Are you hurt bad?" asked Sister softly.

"Well, I'm embarrassed, that's what it is," Nelson said. He smiled in a tired way. "Damn that Charlie."

Natasha had torn a flour sack into long strips that she'd tied together. She wanted Sister to hold the marten stretcher around the lower part of

Nelson's arm while she wrapped the flour-sack strips around it. His arm had been broken. The stretcher would make a splint to keep his arm steady so that the bone would knit together. Then she made a sling for the arm with a pair of Toughboy's jeans and some safety pins, and she was finished.

Nelson fell asleep right away, before he'd even had supper.

# 23

TOUGHBOY SLEPT ON THE FLOOR THAT night so Natasha could sleep in his bunk. She got up early in the morning, before Sister, and made tea. When Sister and Toughboy woke up she was staring at the fire with a cup of tea in her hand.

She didn't answer them when they asked how Nelson was.

Finally she turned to them. "I got to get help," she said.

Toughboy and Sister watched her, waiting for what she'd say next.

"I'm not too worried about that arm," she said. "It's a clean break, just one place. But it seems like he's got some ribs stove in and maybe something beat up inside. You can't tell when they

120

get hurt in their guts what will happen. I can't take him with the dogs the way he is. I'll get Billy to come in with his plane and pick him up. Here's what you kids got to do."

As Natasha explained how to take care of Nelson, she put on each layer of her heavy clothes, talking all the time.

"Don't forget to cut wood every day. It's getting colder now and you don't want to get caught short. Someone got to stay with Nelson all the time so you'll have to forget about the line. I'll be back with Billy in a few days, anyway."

She told Toughboy to bring Nelson's dogs from the willows where they'd been tied up after the accident. The dogs looked surprised that Natasha was hooking them up, but they were polite and well behaved about it.

After the dogs were in their harnesses, she sent Toughboy to the cache for the burlap bag of bait fish so she could take it for dog feed.

She figured it would take two days. She'd head for McGrath because it was closer than their own village, only seventy-five miles.

Natasha put dry meat, pilot crackers, tea, sugar, some of the frozen beans, and a skillet in her pack. That would be her dinner on the trail and her breakfast and lunch, too. She put a sleeping bag and the pack and the dog feed in the sled, and then she covered the whole load with a heavy canvas tarp.

After she had tied the tarp down, she stood on the runners, pulled up her hood and called to the dogs. "All right!" They looked at her over their shoulders for just a second and then they lunged forward. The sled runners broke loose from the ice and they were off.

Charlie stared after the team for a moment and then seemed to remember that he was the leader. He raced to catch up with them and got ahead of them just as they went over the bank.

When they couldn't see Natasha and the team anymore, Toughboy and Sister looked at each other. Everything had happened so fast.

It felt very odd to have Natasha gone.

But it was only for a few days, and nothing could go wrong.

# 24

NELSON DIDN'T WAKE UP UNTIL NAtasha had gone and the sun was just turning the sky pink. Sister thought maybe he'd slept so late because he'd been awake most of the night. Maybe his arm had been hurting him.

Toughboy brought him a steaming cup of coffee. Sister put a rolled sleeping bag behind his back so he could sit up a little.

"Natasha said you shouldn't move much, Nelson. Does it hurt?"

They felt a little shy with him.

The old man grinned. "I feel pretty foolish, lying here in this woman's nightgown." He frowned at Toughboy. "How do I look, boy? Do you think the color becomes me?"

Toughboy bit his lip and tried not to laugh. Nelson did look pretty silly all right.

Nelson looked around for Natasha. "Where's the old lady?"

Toughboy and Sister looked at each other. They didn't know that Natasha hadn't told Nelson what she was going to do.

What if he got mad?

Finally Sister said, "Natasha took your dogs and went to McGrath this morning. She said she'd get Billy Cross to pick you up in the plane."

Nelson's face looked like it was having a conversation with itself as he thought about what Sister had just said. His eyebrows jumped around, he frowned and twisted his lips.

At last he sputtered, unbelievingly, "She left me to take care of two kids? I don't know nothing about taking care of kids!"

Toughboy and Sister couldn't think what to say to that.

"We're supposed to take care of you, not you're supposed to take care of us," said Toughboy at last.

Nelson looked at Toughboy blankly. "You're

supposed to take care of me. That's a good one. How old are you, anyway?"

"Fourteen," said Toughboy, lying.

Nelson gave him a sideways look. "Eleven," said Toughboy.

Nelson scratched his chin where white bristles had sprouted overnight, and then looked like he'd suddenly thought of something that worried him.

"Hell, that Charlie ain't going to listen to her. She'll have a time with him. He only listens to me."

He swallowed half the cup of coffee with one gulp, without paying any attention to how hot it was. Toughboy winced and looked to see if Sister had noticed.

Nelson was still arguing with himself. "Still, she's been across these hills a hundred times with a bigger team. 'Course, she was a damn sight younger. But she don't seem any older now. She's still tough."

He looked suddenly at Toughboy. "What's the temperature?"

"I don't know," said Toughboy. He moved to the window to look at the thermometer, and noticed that the frost was thick again. He was surprised at the temperature. Things had happened so fast he hadn't noticed the cold this morning.

"Twenty-five below," he said to Nelson.

"Hmm," said Nelson. "If we're lucky it won't get any colder. Turn on the radio, will you?"

They listened to the messages and the weather report. They weren't going to be lucky. There was a cold front moving in and they were predicting a bad cold spell.

Nelson looked around the cabin a little nervously. "This old place has seen better days. How much wood you got?"

Toughboy shrugged to show that it was enough.

Nelson shook his head. "You're going to burn a lot of wood in this place when this cold hits. These old cabins are full of holes."

"I'll cut some more today," said Toughboy.

Nelson looked at him hard. "You had much experience cutting wood? You're pretty small."

Sister knew that Toughboy hated it when people said he was small. So she said, "He's very strong for his age."

Nelson smiled his crazy smile. "That's what they say about me, too!"

While he got dressed to do his outdoor chores, Toughboy was thinking about Natasha out there in the woods by herself. He wondered how fast she could go with those three dogs.

"Will there be a good trail to McGrath?" he asked Nelson.

"There's a cat trail all the way to McGrath that they bulldozed when there was big mining camps out here. It'll be grown over with willows some, but not too bad. Down in the valleys it might be drifted, but when she gets up on the tops of the hills it will be good. She's done it many times before. Won't be much different now. Unless this bad cold catches up with her."

"If she had a snow machine," said Toughboy, "she could make it in one day."

Nelson made a face. "Shows how much you know. That's uphill most of the way. A snow machine's not much good uphill, especially if there's any drifts. She's a lot better off with dogs this time. A lot better."

Toughboy wound his scarf around his face. "Do you have a snow machine, Nelson?"

"No. I hate them things. If you break down, where are you then? What if you run out of gas? With dogs you always make it, even if it takes longer." He jabbed his finger at Toughboy's surprised face. "And going fast ain't so much. You freeze your face and your feet, going so fast, and you can't stop and run behind a snow machine the way you can a dogsled. No way to warm up. And you don't see any dog teams getting stuck in overflow, do you? Soon as a dog feels water under his feet he stops. No snow machine can do that."

Toughboy had never heard anyone talk this way. Everyone he knew thought snow machines were much better than dog teams. Daddy had gotten rid of his dogs as soon as he could buy a snow machine.

He thought about himself, standing tall on the runners behind a long team of huskies, cracking a whip over their heads. He'd go faster and farther than anyone. Maybe he'd race in the North American. He'd win, too. John Silas, Jr., the North American Sled Dog Champion.

But he was all dressed in his outside gear and he was getting so hot in the cabin he had to go out or he'd die. He'd have to talk to Nelson about this later.

# 25

SISTER COOKED SOME OF THE DRIED apples for Nelson's breakfast, but he didn't eat very much. While she did that Toughboy brought in some snow to melt, and then he brought two buckets of water from the river. Sister put on her outside clothes so she could help with the wood cutting. She looked out the window while she tied her mukluks.

Suddenly the woodpile didn't look very big.

Toughboy and Sister cut down three spruce trees. They limbed them and then they cut each tree into five sections so they could put them in the sled and drag them home. It took them three trips. Whenever they got back to the cabin they'd warm up for a few minutes and see if Nelson needed anything. He still hadn't tried to get up, so Sister thought he must be hurting pretty badly.

When the wood was hauled home Toughboy and Sister were tired. But the wood still had to be sawed into shorter chunks to fit into the wood stove, and some had to be split and some had to be cut into kindling.

The temperature stayed the same all day, but when the sun began to go down it dropped again. There was heavy frost on the door hinges now, and the frost on the windows had climbed higher every hour.

Sister brought in the wood they'd already split the day before and piled it up against the wall by the door.

Nelson smiled at her. "You're a hard-working little girl, aren't you? How old are you?"

"I'm nine," said Sister. "How old are you?"

"I'll be seventy-nine in April," said the old man.

Sister stared into his eyes for a minute, trying to think what seventy-nine would feel like. It was hard enough even to think about how nine was different from eight, or to imagine what it would be like to be ten. Seventy-nine was too hard to imagine.

"What's your name?" he asked.

"Sister." He seemed to be waiting for more, so she said, "Annie Laurie Silas."

"Annie Laurie is the name of a song."

"I know," said Sister. "Mamma told me she liked that song. They used to play it in the dance hall when she was little. On the violin. But I never did hear it."

"Well, I can't sing it for you," Nelson said with a laugh. "But it's a pretty song." He looked at her. "It's a kind of sad song. Looks like it was a good song to name you for. You have a serious look to you."

Sister sat on the rickety chair by Natasha's bed. "Is Nelson your first name or your last name?"

"Well, my folks named me Einar Nelson Dinenberg. But I thought Einar was a sissy name, and not American enough. They were born in the old country, you see, and I didn't like to be taken for a greenhorn. So I just went by Nelson."

Sister nodded. Einar was a pretty strange name, and she could imagine a boy hating it.

"How come Natasha's got you out here with her? Where's your folks?"

"They're dead," Sister said. "We're living with Natasha now."

Nelson nodded his head thoughtfully. "That's a tough old woman. Must be no pleasing her!"

Sister didn't say anything. But she was beginning to like this old man a lot.

Mutt was barking outdoors. Sister ran to the window to see if her moose had come back.

But it wasn't the moose. It was Charlie, trotting up the trail in the bright sunshine, frost all over his muzzle. He scratched at the door fast and hard, demanding to come in.

Sister opened the door, and Charlie raced to Nelson's bed. He jumped up on Nelson's chest and began licking his face.

"Oh," gasped Sister. She was sure Charlie would hurt Nelson's arm or ribs, but Nelson didn't show any sign that Charlie had hurt him.

"You left that old woman, didn't you?" Nelson bellowed happily. "What's she going to do without a leader, answer me that? You're spoiled!"

The old man was so happy to have Charlie there, and Charlie was so happy to be there, that Sister had to laugh. That little dog had the laughingest face she'd ever seen.

"Nelson, how will Natasha manage without a leader?" Sister asked.

"Don't give it a thought." He bent toward her and whispered, "We just let Charlie *think* he's the leader." Then he winked at her.

Toughboy came banging in with the last load of wood. The cold air billowed into the room in white swirls. Sister hated the rush of cold.

Nelson slowly put both feet on the floor. Charlie jumped down off the bed, wagging his whole body, ready to go wherever Nelson was going.

Nelson asked Sister to get his shoepacks and his parka for him. He moved carefully, as if he were very stiff. When he saw her looking at him with concern he smiled. "I feel like I been clubbed with a two-by-four," he said. Nelson couldn't put his broken arm in the parka sleeve, so he tucked the sling inside and zipped up the parka over it.

When Nelson came back from the outhouse he sat back down on the bed with a groan. Toughboy was up on the stool hanging his clothes over the fire.

"Well, I looked at that woodpile," Nelson said, looking up at Toughboy. "You're a pretty good man in the woods."

Toughboy's face felt very hot. A pretty good man in the woods. A good man in the woods.

"How old did you say you was?" asked Nelson.

Toughboy's voice caught in his throat and gave a little croak. "Eleven," he said.

Nelson nodded his head and smiled. "Eleven," he said to himself.

When someone praised Toughboy he always felt as if he were going to laugh or cry or do something stupid. It wasn't the sort of thing that happened very often so he didn't have many chances to get used to it.

He wished something would happen to Nelson again, so he, Toughboy, could save him. He'd do anything. He'd jump in after him if Nelson were drowning, even if he couldn't swim. He'd be brave and daring like the old miners, and make jokes while he was swimming to shore.

Walking seemed to wear Nelson out, and he lay down on the bed again.

"You know, when we worked out at the camps we used to cut twenty cords of that pole wood a

135

day. That's wood for the boilers, you know. Then I'd walk the seven miles over to Poorman for the dance, get a little drunk, and walk back again. Didn't think nothing of it."

Toughboy looked at Nelson in despair. Twenty cords of wood a day? He'd never be able to cut twenty cords a day.

There was no way you could keep up with these old people.

# 26

IT WAS VERY LATE THAT NIGHT WHEN they finished everything that needed to be done —the cooking and the dishes and the washing up, and drying their clothes.

At last they filled the stove full of wood, shut the dampers, and went to sleep. They were as tired as they'd ever been, and Sister's legs ached as if they were on fire.

But Toughboy didn't sleep long. Cold crept into his sleeping bag and wrenched him awake a few hours later. He could see his breath.

He climbed down out of his bunk and opened up the dampers in the stove. The fire started blazing right away, and the flames flickered through the damper holes in the stove front and lit up the whole room. It was a warm feeling to have firelight dancing on the walls of the cabin in the middle of the night. Now they would have to keep the dampers open to keep the cabin warm.

Toughboy woke again in a few hours. The fire had burned itself out and he was stiff with cold. He put his parka and shoepacks on with numb, awkward fingers. His fingers were so cold that he dropped the whole box of matches onto the dirt floor.

At last Toughboy had the birchbark blazing and he shivered hard, waiting by the stove for the kindling to start snapping.

The sides of the stove were cold to the touch, and it was as though he'd only imagined the fire in there a few hours ago.

Sister had made a ball of herself in her sleeping bag. She must be cold, too.

He saw that Nelson was awake. His sleeping bag was pulled up to his chin.

Toughboy felt ashamed that he'd let the fire go out. "I'm trying to get this fire going. I opened it up too far, and it burned out on me, I guess."

Nelson smiled. "Happens to the best of us," he said. "I've got a feeling you're going to have to run that stove wide open for the next few days. The bottom must have dropped out of the thermometer tonight."

Toughboy had to get up every two hours for the rest of the night to put more wood in the stove. He never let it go out again. He'd wake up just as the wood was gone and there were lots of red coals left. All he had to do was stir up the coals with the poker and put more wood on, and the fire would blaze up again.

He wondered how he knew exactly when to wake up.

When Sister got up in the morning there was ice in the water bucket, and when she lit the two kerosene lamps she could see that a thick frost had almost covered the windows. There were frosted places all over the walls, and the door was nearly solid with frost. The nailheads in the ceiling were covered with white fur, and her sleeping bag had frozen to the wall.

The cold was out there, waiting to get them, and it was creeping under the door and in through the cracks.

The black cold was giving her a lonesome feeling, so she turned on the radio. Maybe there would be a message from Natasha this morning. She pulled on her jeans and shirt as fast as she could. Then she put on her wool socks and shoepacks and her snow pants and parka. She felt that she could never get warm enough.

She made coffee for Nelson, and put the cup on the little table next to his bed so that he'd have it as soon as he woke up. She poured herself a cup, too. Then she put her feet up on one of the gas boxes next to the stove and wrapped her hands around her hot cup. She put her face into the steam to drink in that heat too.

She looked at Toughboy. He was still sleeping hard. Then she noticed the woodpile against the wall. The wood was nearly gone. All the wood she'd brought in yesterday. How could they have burned that much?

She felt suddenly frantic at the thought of everything that must be done, right away. They must cut more wood, and bring it in to warm by the fire, and they must melt more snow, and make breakfast, and then lunch and then dinner, and put more and more and more wood into the fire. There would be no end to it.

Nelson turned over and opened his eyes. He leaned over to pat Charlie who was lying on the floor next to his bed. Then Nelson smiled at Sister.

"Better let Toughboy sleep awhile. He's been up all night tending that fire. It's mighty cold out there."

"Your coffee's there," said Sister. She was so glad that Nelson was awake. The cold wasn't so bad with Nelson to talk to. He was so quiet and sure of things.

Nelson picked up the cup and then made a funny face. He put his lips to the cup to be sure. "Stone cold," he said.

Sister couldn't believe it. That hot cup of coffee had cooled in just a few minutes. She laid her hand against the wall above the little table. A dull cold seeped through the walls. There was no way to stop it.

She poured him another cup of coffee and they listened to the radio. It was fifty-five below in McGrath. Natasha was caught in the bad weather.

"Nelson, what will Natasha do?"

"Oh, don't worry, little girl. There's a lot of cabins between here and McGrath. She could have holed up in one of those. Or she just *siwashed*. She's done that before.

"But this weather's too cold for my dogs. I hope she doesn't try to push them. If she's got some idea I'm going to die or something she might try to get into McGrath, and she'll hurt them dogs."

Sister saw that Nelson was more worried about his dogs than about Natasha or himself.

"What's '*siwash*,' Nelson?"

"That's what you call it when you have to stay out at night. Most people just cut some spruce boughs and make a sort of shelter with that. Put some more boughs on the ground to sleep on. You make a big fire close by. That'll keep you alive when you got to sleep out. But you got to be careful you don't get too close to that fire. Some people creep closer and closer when they're asleep, trying to stay warm, and they burn holes in their boots or clothes.

"But up in Eskimo country they do things different. They dig down into the snow. It's warm under the snow. Don't need a fire under there. It's lots better than trying to keep a fire going. That'll wear you out."

He put his cup down. "Go check and see what the temperature is here."

The ice was too thick on the window to see the thermometer, so Sister took the flashlight hanging by the door and went out to read it. Their thermometer read forty-six below. Not as cold as McGrath.

She looked up into the cold sky. She'd never seen it so black, or so full of stars. It looked as if all the stars had hardened and sharpened and brightened with the cold. They frightened her.

When Sister went back inside, a billow of cold air rushed in with her and crept into all the corners, though she tried to shut the door as fast as she could. "Forty-six," she said.

Nelson nodded. "McGrath is lower than we are. It's always colder in the flats than it is in the hills. If she stays on the ridges it'll be warmer than forty-six. That's not too bad."

Toughboy jerked awake when the cold air hit him. He climbed out of his bunk and staggered to the stove before he realized that the lamps were lit and they were already awake. "We got to go get more wood," he said to Sister.

## ✳✴ 27 ✴✳

SISTER MADE THEM OATMEAL AND THEN
she toasted some bread on the top of the stove.

They ate the oatmeal with brown sugar. When
they tried to pour milk out of the can they found
it had turned to slush. Sister put the can on top
of the stove to thaw, but they were so hungry
they couldn't wait and they ate the oatmeal without milk.

There was a pink glow coming in through the
frost on the windows, just enough to show that
it was daylight but not enough to brighten up
the cabin. It made Sister feel closed in when the
windows were frosted up and the room was dark.

While Toughboy was getting water Sister tried
to scrape some of the frost away so that sunlight

would come in. Toughboy came in to warm up. His cheeks were bright, fiery red from the cold, and his eyelashes were white with frost. He huddled close to the stove and watched Sister scrape at the window. It was a thick and sullen frost. It would never come off. Sister was impatient to let the sun into the dark room.

She poured some of the hot water from the teakettle onto a rag and held the rag against the window to melt the frost.

There was a terrible sound, like a rifle shot, and the window split into a dozen pieces like a spider web. The biggest piece fell with a jangle to the floor. The cold and the light came pouring in at once.

Nelson swung his long legs over the side of Natasha's bed and threw his sleeping bag over the window. "Nails," he hollered.

Toughboy handed him the can of nails from the shelf. "Hold it," snapped Nelson. "Hold the nail up for me." Toughboy held the nail as Nelson whacked it with a piece of firewood. That didn't drive the nail in very far so Nelson yelled for a hammer.

Toughboy knew exactly where the hammer

was, though he was sure if it had been an ordinary day he wouldn't have remembered. While Toughboy held the nails in place Nelson hammered them in all around the sleeping bag with his one good arm. That stopped the worst of the cold from coming in.

"Get me some cardboard boxes," Nelson told Toughboy.

Toughboy brought back from the cache two of the boxes they'd brought food in. Nelson told him to flatten one out, and they hammered the cardboard over the sleeping bag. Then he told Toughboy to take the other box and do the same thing outdoors. And then the window was fixed and there was no more cold air coming in the awful hole.

Nelson limped back to his bed, and lay down again. Toughboy stirred the coals, and then he put more wood in the stove and opened the dampers. The room was already as cold as it had been when he'd let the fire go out. If they relaxed their guard for a minute the cold would shove in and take over. They had to fight it all the time.

# 28

SISTER LAY ON HER BUNK AND HID HER
head in her arms. She was ashamed to have done
such a stupid thing, and she was grieving for the
window. With only one window left, the cabin
was dark and gloomy.

Then she remembered that it was daylight,
and that the sun would be down again in just a
few hours. They had wood to cut. They always
had to race the darkness and get the wood cut
while the sun was up.

It was a beautiful pink and white day, the cold
white sun shining through the cold haze and
touching the frost on every tree.

Toughboy thought if he lay down on the trail

he would be dead in a few hours on this beautiful day.

He was tired and his eyes ached and his throat was hoarse when he tried to talk, but still they must cut wood, and they couldn't stop until three trees were sawed up and split. When that was finished the wood must be carried in.

The door was being very difficult. The bottom had frosted badly and the hinges were filled with frost, and the cold was seeping in around the frame.

Sister would open and close the door. Toughboy would kick the door, and Sister would open it up just enough for him to come in and then she'd close it very fast so that too much cold couldn't come in. Toughboy would drop his armload of wood by the wall, and then she'd open the door quickly and shut it quickly so he could get another load.

Toughboy dropped the wood much more carelessly than he did when Natasha was there.

Sister straightened the woodpile so that the pieces of wood lay in neat rows.

Nelson laughed at her. "Isn't that just like a woman," he said.

Sister felt proud to be called a woman, so she smiled at Nelson.

When all the wood was stacked inside the house Toughboy climbed up into his bunk and slept again until Sister had made the cheese sandwiches for their supper.

Nelson told Sister to bring all his outdoor clothes. He was going to get dressed. When he had all his winter gear on, except his over-parka, he gave Sister the other sleeping bag on his bed and told her to put it over the door. The door had too many cracks and they'd have to cover it.

She stood on a stool and hammered the sleeping bag into the top of the door frame. It was very hard to get in and out of the door without disturbing the sleeping bag, but too much cold was coming in through the door frame and under the door.

Nelson assured her that he'd be even warmer just sleeping with his parka and snow pants on than he would in that granny gown and sleeping bag.

When Sister went outside to throw out the dishwater, the northern lights had bent and fanned

and stretched all the way down to the river ice.
A million pale bars of pink and green and blue
arched and shimmered to silent music.

Suddenly Sister realized that she hadn't seen
Mutt all evening.

# 29

SISTER THOUGHT AS HARD AS SHE could. Just before she'd broken the window Mutt had scratched at the door the way he always did when he wanted to go out. That was the last time she'd seen him.

But that was hours ago and he was never gone long. Something must have happened to him. He could have been kicked by a moose, too, or fallen through the ice or been killed by a wolf.

"You don't think he'd try to follow Natasha, do you?" Nelson asked.

Toughboy and Sister didn't think so. When Daddy had given up his team he'd unsnapped Mutt's chain and said, "There you go. You're retired."

Mutt had just quietly taken up his job as watchdog, and he seldom went off by himself. He was old, after all, older than Toughboy.

Toughboy felt heavy and sluggish, as if he were sick. He was so tired. But they had to look for Mutt. He was hurt or he would have been back.

"Did you ever take him with you when you checked the traps?" asked Nelson.

"No, Natasha said you shouldn't have dog-smell on your trapline trail. She was afraid he'd try to steal the bait, too. And get caught."

As soon as Toughboy said those words they knew that was what had happened. Mutt was caught in a trap.

He might have frozen to death by now.

Sister began to take her clothes down from the lines over the stove. Toughboy began to dress again, too.

His clothes hadn't had time to dry completely. Nelson stopped him. "Take my things," he said to Toughboy. "They're dry." He took off his winter gear and wrapped himself up in Sister's sleeping bag.

Toughboy hung his damp things back up and put on Nelson's big socks and mukluks and snow pants. He had to roll the pants legs up two turns because Nelson's legs were so long.

"Oh, hurry," said Sister. She took the flashlight from the wall and went outside.

The cold was sharp and beautiful. A slice of icy white moon made long black tree shadows on the snow. A cold white curtain of northern lights tumbled and slid about far away in the sky over the mountains.

Sister said she'd go on the short trail and Toughboy could search the other trail. They'd save time if they went in different directions. Toughboy should take the flashlight because his trail was darker, through the woods.

"No," he said quickly. Toughboy hated the woods at night. He searched his mind for a good enough reason to give Sister.

"Natasha said when it's cold you never go anyplace by yourself. You always got to have a partner."

Sister looked at him for a moment. "Maybe you're right."

They decided to check the short trail first. With their hoods pulled forward to cover their faces they couldn't see anything except the trail under their feet. They couldn't hear anything except their own harsh breathing and the loud *crunch, crunch* of their mukluks on the frozen packed snow.

They had to stop and push back their hoods a little way off their faces so they could call for Mutt. Then they'd stand very still and listen for his answer. The cold slashed at their lungs and faces.

At the third trap Toughboy heard a sound. He strained to see deep into the woods by the trail, and he saw what he'd always feared to see. Tall and menacing, and bent—it was a woodsman.

Toughboy saw its evil eyes, and a scream choked his throat. Sister tried to see what Toughboy was looking at. She glanced quickly at his face. His eyes were wild and terrified. Her heart began to thump wildly.

"What?" she whispered fiercely.

"A woodsman," he whispered back.

"Oh, Toughboy." She smiled with relief. "You scared me. You know there's no such thing." As she spoke the woodsman shifted, melted back into a skinny spruce tree, bent with frost.

"I jokes," said Toughboy weakly, still staring at the tree.

It seemed to grow colder every moment. Even Nelson's heavy clothes weren't enough to keep Toughboy warm. The cold found every rip, every tiny hole, every place the fabric was weak, and it crept into those places.

He was too tired to stay warm. On his chest there was a place, a quiet little patch of cold, and it began to spread up over his shoulders and down his back.

He was beginning to stumble. There was a cold hard knot in his stomach that ached from trying to stay warm, from holding his body tense against the cold.

At the very end of the short line there was a sharp turn in the trail that led up the hill and over the top. It was just around this turn that they found Mutt.

He didn't bark or jump when they came upon him. He was so quiet that they might even have passed him by if they hadn't been shining the light on every trap they came to.

His eyes glowed in the glare of the flashlight, and he turned his head away from the light. He hung his head down, as if he knew he'd done wrong to go so far away. As if he felt stupid to be so greedy as to try to eat the bait. As if he wouldn't blame them if they walked away and left him in the trap.

It was his left foot. He'd stood up on his hind legs to get the bait, and his left front foot had been caught. He'd pulled the trap off the pole so that he could sit down, but still his paw was up in the air, held tight in the jaws of the trap.

Mutt looked like a boy raising his hand for permission to speak.

Sister was afraid to look at his foot. She was sure it would be bloody and awful. Maybe he'd tried to chew his paw off like a marten.

A hatred for the traps filled Sister. She wanted to smash things, tear things up, break something. Her anger made her hands shake.

Toughboy snapped the trap with a stick and Mutt slowly lowered his paw to the ground. Then he looked at Sister sadly and gave his tail a small wag.

Sister tried to lift Mutt up to carry him home but he was too heavy.

Toughboy groaned. "How stupid we are. Why didn't we bring the toboggan?"

They watched as Mutt limped a few feet.

"He'll have to walk. We can't carry him," said Toughboy.

When they reached the next trap Sister stopped and looked at it for a moment. Then she broke off a willow branch from beside the trail and snapped the trap. She hit it so hard that the chain that held it to the pole broke, too.

Mutt stopped in the trail to look back at her, and Toughboy stared at her with surprise.

When he saw the look on her face he decided not to say anything at all.

On the way home Sister snapped every single trap on the short line with that stick.

# ✳✳ 30 ✳✳

BY THE TIME THEY GOT TO THE CABIN
Mutt wasn't limping anymore. It wasn't until
they got him inside that they saw how badly he
was hurt.

Nelson called Mutt over to the bed and looked
at his foot very carefully. Then he banged it
lightly against the table leg next to his bed. It
made a thumping sound, like a block of wood.
"Frozen solid," said Nelson.

"What should we do?" asked Sister anxiously.
She and Toughboy were crouched next to the
stove, still cold deep down in their bones.

Nelson looked troubled. "Well, out at the
mines we used to rub frozen feet in kerosene. I

don't know about a dog, though," he said doubtfully.

"Natasha said to use snow," said Toughboy.

Nelson snorted. "That's damned stupid, if you ask me."

"Maybe warm water, like they told us at school," said Sister. Nelson threw out his hands to show that he didn't know a better way.

Toughboy felt sick. "Will his foot have to be cut off?"

Nelson shook his head. "I just don't know." Sister had a feeling that Nelson felt as bad about Mutt as they did. "I'm afraid he's going to be hurting, though. Damn, I hate to see an animal suffer."

He looked at Sister. "Look in my sled bag and get that bottle of whiskey. They used to use whiskey in the old days when someone had to have a tooth taken out."

"Or a bullet taken out," said Toughboy. He had seen that in a western movie at the community hall.

Nelson told Sister to put a little of the whiskey in a bowl of milk and give it to Mutt. She put the bowl in front of Mutt but his ears shot up and he looked at it suspiciously.

"It smells awful," said Sister.

Mutt moved away from the bowl, so they gave up that idea. Sister tried to warm Mutt's paw with a wet, hot towel, but Mutt kept pulling his paw away so he could lick it.

There was nothing they could do to ease his pain. Toughboy thought how his cheek had stung when he'd frostbitten it. That was just a little place. What would a whole foot feel like?

"Stupid dog," he said angrily, because he was so sad.

That night Sister dreamed of Mutt, lots of Mutts, hanging in the trees and trapped by one foot. In her dream she could feel the terrible pain in each paw, and she woke up with tears on her face.

## ❊❊ 31 ❊❊

TOUGHBOY HAD TO GET UP EVERY FEW hours to tend the fire again that night. Mutt was sleeping in the bed with Sister, inside the sleeping bag, and Charlie was sleeping with Nelson.

At night they moved the beds away from the walls and into the center of the room, closer to the fire, but it was still hard to sleep. The cabin just wouldn't get warm enough.

They had all begun to wear their snow pants and jackets indoors.

They stayed warm when they were moving around and doing their chores, but they were never really warm enough when they were lying still. Then the cold would soak into their clothes and keep them half awake.

If they couldn't keep going, if they couldn't keep fire in the stove, they would freeze. That white icy breath would keep breathing and breathing on them and they'd be frozen hard and stiff.

When Sister woke she got the flashlight before she even lit the lamp and she looked at Mutt's paw. It was puffed up, and he whimpered when she touched it. It felt hot to her hand. Sister told Mutt to stay on the bed and she got up to light the lamps and stoke the fire. Then she turned on the radio.

Maybe there would be a message from Natasha today. Maybe she'd made it to McGrath. She made coffee and brought it to Nelson as soon as he stirred. Sister saw that Nelson was having a hard time sitting up.

As he drank his coffee he listened intently to the radio. When the messages were over, and the weather report was finished, he snapped off the radio and lay back down wearily. It was sixty-five below in McGrath.

"Where do you think Natasha is?" Sister asked.

"Oh, holed up someplace, most likely. You don't need to worry about her." Nelson rubbed the bristles on his chin. That made a sound like sandpaper.

Toughboy was awake now. He was thinking about summer.

He couldn't even remember what warm felt like. When he was warm again, really warm, he'd pay attention to what it felt like. He'd never again not notice that he was warm. He'd never get cross in the summer when the sun was overhead all day and his clothes stuck to him. He'd never, ever say it was too hot.

He climbed down from his bunk to stand by the fire.

Nelson put his coffee cup on the table and lay down again. "I'll tell you kids what. You'd better get a shovel and pile up the snow as deep as you can all around the cabin. That will help keep this place warmer."

Toughboy nodded. He was clumsy with tiredness.

The wood was nearly gone. They had to cut three more trees today, maybe more, maybe more. Toughboy stared at the dirt floor under his feet and knew it was impossible. He could never be as tough as the long-ago people. The old-time way was too hard for him.

"How's the dog today, girlie?" asked Nelson kindly.

Sister told him about the swelling and the hotness in Mutt's foot. Nelson nodded.

Sister ran her hand gently over Mutt's head and back. Mutt looked at her lovingly and thumped his tail.

Nelson squinted to bring Mutt into focus.

"It don't seem like it's bothering him too much," he said.

After Sister had cooked breakfast she and Toughboy got ready to cut wood. The wood was so important that Sister didn't clean up the dishes or tidy the cabin. She could do that when the wood was in.

Nelson didn't want any breakfast at all.

"What was the temperature in McGrath this morning?" asked Toughboy.

"Sixty-five below," said Nelson.

"Wow!" said Toughboy.

Maybe it would never stop. Maybe it would just keep getting colder and colder. "How long will this last, Nelson?"

"No way to tell," said Nelson. "I seen it last this cold for weeks. You just can't tell."

He looked at Toughboy. "We need some birch. Birch burns hotter and longer than spruce. You might be able to sleep more than a couple of hours at a time."

Toughboy nodded. "I could cut one of the birch trees back of the outhouse."

Nelson smiled at Toughboy. "If I'd ever had a partner as reliable as you I'd probably be a rich man now."

# ✳✳ 32 ✳✳

SISTER HELPED TOUGHBOY WITH THE wood all day. They could only work outdoors for a short while, and then they'd have to come in and thaw out their numb fingers and stinging faces. Their scarves would freeze solid over their mouths and rub against their faces miserably.

Getting cold was always the same. Their thumbs would get cold first and then their wrists. There was a spot between the tops of their mittens and the cuffs of their parkas that always came uncovered when they worked. When that place got cold it stung and burned worse than any other place.

The bone under the eyebrows was another bad place. You could never keep that place warm.

When it got cold it ached with a dull, horrible ache and would ache long after you'd gotten warm.

Sister would get Nelson what he needed when they came inside, and would bring water to Mutt while Toughboy tended the fire.

Once when they came in Nelson had made them a pot of cocoa. It was the most delicious cocoa they'd ever tasted. It had cinnamon in it. But Nelson moved more slowly than before, and they could see that it had been a terrible effort to do that for them.

Sometimes when they came in Toughboy would fall asleep by the fire. He was so tired now from getting up in the nights it seemed like he fell asleep any time he stopped moving.

They shoveled the snow up around the house as high as they could, and then they cut down the birch tree.

It was so cold that the birch split in two with the lightest blow of Toughboy's ax.

Finally, when they'd finished splitting the wood, Toughboy got into his bunk and fell asleep with his mukluks and everything on. Sister fed the birch into the stove and opened both dampers.

The wood was cold and wouldn't put out much heat. Finally it began to blaze and it threw out a very comforting, steady heat.

Sister fell asleep herself, and woke to find the sides of the stove glowing red-hot. They were so red they looked as if you could see through the metal. Sparks were jumping from the open damper on the stove door.

Sister didn't know what to do. She shook Nelson awake.

"Whoa," said Nelson. "You're going to set that chimney on fire!"

Toughboy jumped up when he felt the heat from the stove. He looked helplessly at Nelson.

Now the stovepipe was glowing as red as the stove sides.

"Sister, close those dampers," yelled Nelson. Sister had to put her gloves on to turn the handle on the stovepipe damper. She was terrified. If she fell against the stove that red-hot metal would sear her and she'd be horribly burned.

A strange sound shook the stove. "Too late," yelled Nelson. The chimney was roaring and shooting sparks. With his good arm Nelson grabbed the bucket of water from the stove.

"Open the stove," he hollered at Sister, "and stand back!"

Sister wrenched the stove door open and sheets of flame roared out to lick her face. Nelson threw the bucket of water into the stove and the noise died down suddenly. The water turned to steam with a hiss, and smoke filled the room. The stove was suddenly silent, and then it snapped and popped as if the cold water had shocked it. Black, syrupy creosote ran down the sides of the stove-pipe.

The room grew colder in a minute.

They stared at the stove as if it might catch on fire again. "God almighty," said Nelson. "If it ain't one thing and then another."

# ✳✳ 33 ✳✳

SISTER FELT HOT TEARS ON HER CHEEKS.
Now she was crying, like a baby. She buried her
face in Mutt's fur. Why had she fallen asleep, oh,
why had she let the stove get too hot? She just
couldn't do anything right, these last few days.

Nelson didn't say anything about the tears, he
just chuckled. "Well, we needed to clean out
those ashes. Now's our chance."

Sister pinched her lips together and frowned
hard at Nelson. Was he just saying that to make
her feel better?

"Go ahead, boy, rake all those ashes out into
the bucket. That fire will burn a whole lot better
now."

Maybe he *had* said it so she wouldn't feel bad, but she felt better anyway. It was true that they had to get those ashes out. She smiled at Nelson and he smiled back, his silly smile, the one that nearly touched his ears.

The stove was full of wet ashes and Toughboy had to carry out four heavy bucket loads and throw them over the bank before the job was finished. Then they started a new fire. They were too tired for supper so they all ate some pilot crackers and drank some tea and went to sleep.

Morning came too soon. It was time for Sister to get up and fix the fire and make the coffee.

She was still tired and so dirty. The whole cabin smelled of smoke and soot from the fire, and she hadn't done the dishes yesterday. There were puddles of sooty water on the table and chairs. Everything was a terrible mess.

She had to get up.

Sister wanted Natasha to come back, she wanted to sleep late, she wanted not to worry about the wood or the cold. She wanted someone to bring her breakfast. She wanted to be a baby. A baby had to do nothing. Everybody loved a baby. They didn't expect anything from a baby.

She tried to make herself get out of her sleeping bag, but her mind was too heavy and she fell back to sleep.

She dreamed that they couldn't move, that she and Toughboy and Nelson were rusted. They couldn't get the wood, they couldn't chop it, they couldn't put it in the stove. Slowly a frozen light filled the room and slowly the room grew colder and colder and they all grew stiff and white, staring at the ceiling and waiting to freeze. In her dream they all had blue eyes, even Toughboy and Sister.

She woke with a jerk and found the room was full of daylight. She'd slept way, way too long, and the fire was nearly out. She pulled herself off the bed and began wearily to rake the coals.

When she had finished making the fire Sister turned on the radio and sliced the bread while Toughboy went to fetch water. She made toast and cooked the oatmeal and made coffee for Nelson. He drank his coffee, but Sister saw that he only pretended to eat his oatmeal. He pushed it around with his spoon and made a hole in the middle so it would look like he'd eaten a lot, but it was only pushed up on the edge of the bowl. That was what she used to do when Mamma gave her Cream of Wheat for breakfast.

Nelson hadn't eaten for a few days. And he was having a hard time getting out of bed, and lying back down.

Sister turned away from the stove and looked at him, lying quietly on the bed. His eyes were closed as he listened to the radio, waiting for the messages.

She walked to the bed and bent over and gave him a hug. He opened his eyes fast and looked startled. Then he smiled. "Don't worry," he said, as if he knew what she was thinking.

And suddenly, there it was. A message. Toughboy dropped the wood he was putting in the stove and stood still to listen.

"For the trappers at Sulatna: Made it to McGrath okay, will send a plane as soon as it warms up. Dogs are fine. Natasha."

She'd done it. Nelson let out a whoop. Sister hugged Toughboy and whirled around the cabin.

She hugged Mutt. Mutt and Charlie began to bark at them, they were all so suddenly loud and silly.

She'd made it. They smiled at each other so hard their faces got tired, and they asked each other a dozen questions no one had the answers to. When had she reached McGrath? Did she have to *siwash?* Was the trail good? Did she hit any overflow?

Toughboy could hardly wait to hear Natasha's stories.

# ☀ 34 ☀

AS SOON AS SHE HAD LIT THE KEROSENE
lamp the next morning, Sister took the flashlight
and went outside to check the temperature.

When she came back into the cabin she heard
the bedsprings squeak and she knew that Nelson
was awake. He was waiting to hear what the
temperature was.

She went to his bed and touched his hand.
"Forty-two, Nelson," she said joyfully. "Billy can
fly today, can't he?"

Nelson settled back into the pillow and smiled
at her. Sister thought he seemed terribly tired
this morning. "Yeah," he said. "Billy can fly."

\* \* \*

It was only an hour after sunrise when they heard, very clear in the morning air, the *whackety-whackety* sound of a plane.

Toughboy rushed to the riverbank and looked in every direction for a sign of Billy's plane. Then he saw it.

It was a moment before he realized what it was. "It's a helicopter," he yelled. "It's a helicopter! A helicopter!"

A green helicopter.

Natasha had brought the air rescue for Nelson.

The helicopter dropped lower and lower onto the frozen river in front of the cabin, and the snow blew up in all directions. Toughboy couldn't see a thing.

The engine stopped, and the snow settled around the helicopter. Toughboy had never seen a helicopter close up. It was big.

The pilot, a tall soldier in winter gear, climbed out. He was very serious, all business, just like in the movies.

He ran around to the side of the helicopter and opened the door. Another soldier hopped out, and then they pulled out a stretcher and a bag.

There was no sign of Natasha.

The soldiers started up the trail toward the cabin. Toughboy stood on the bank staring down at them. He had a feeling Nelson wasn't going to like all this fuss.

Nelson looked very flustered as the soldiers bustled into the cabin. They seemed to take up a lot of space and the cabin seemed very crowded.

"Where's the old woman?" asked Nelson.

The tall soldier had wrapped a sort of bandage around Nelson's arm, and was pumping up a rubber ball.

"She's going to be laid up for a week or so, sir," the soldier said. Toughboy had never heard anyone call someone "sir." It sounded so respectful, like Nelson was someone very important.

"What happened?" asked Nelson, looking grim.

"She frostbit a couple of toes, sir," said the soldier. "But she'll be fine. She's tough as nails, that old lady."

Nelson looked at Toughboy and Sister and laughed.

The other soldier took the bandage thing off Nelson's arm and wrote something on his clipboard. "She told us she did okay until she came to where the drifts were bad," he said. "Then she had to walk in front of the dogs to break trail for them. That tired her out so she couldn't make it to a cabin she had in mind. She had to sleep out. That was the night it got so cold. She said she was so tired she kept falling asleep and then the fire would go out. That's how she froze her toes. The next day she made it to the cabin and the trapper made her stay there. He came into McGrath by snow machine and called us. We picked her up yesterday morning and took her to McGrath. We were experiencing pretty bad icing conditions so we had to wait till today to get you, sir."

Toughboy and Sister thought of Natasha out in that terrible cold, too tired to keep the fire going.

"Where's my dogs?" asked Nelson.

The tall soldier laughed. "They're in McGrath, sir, with the old woman. She made sure we took those dogs with us in the helicopter. She said she didn't want to answer to you if she left them behind. And those dogs didn't like that ride one bit, either. And neither did she. She cussed us out all the way into McGrath."

Toughboy and Sister knew just how Natasha would have sounded, and they were a little embarrassed. But Nelson settled back into the pillow and smiled. "That's the old lady, all right," he said happily.

The soldier looked at Toughboy. "She said to tell you kids to spring the traps and close up camp."

Nelson scowled. "It's too damn cold for you kids to go out there and spring that short line. You nearly froze yourselves last time when you went after that dog."

Toughboy bit his lip and looked at Sister. They hadn't told Nelson what Sister had done the night that Mutt was caught in the trap.

Sister felt silly, now, remembering how wild she'd been, how she'd slammed the stick into each trap, hoping she would break it.

"I sprang all the traps already, the night Mutt was lost. I got mad," she said.

Nelson turned his head to look at her carefully. He was quiet a moment, and then he smiled his biggest smile. "Lord, you're a pistol, ain't you? Butter wouldn't melt in your mouth and then slam, bam, you up and spring all the traps."

Toughboy was trying hard not to laugh. Sister's face turned pink and she wasn't sure what to say.

"Well," Nelson said, "that's that. Pack up what you want to take home, and lock things up."

"We still have to spring the traps on the first mile of the long line," said Sister.

"I'll do that right now," said Toughboy.

Toughboy and Sister put on their heavy clothes and the two soldiers examined Nelson carefully. They didn't pay any attention to his arm, but ran their fingers over his belly and pulled up his eyelids and listened to his heart. They asked Nelson a dozen questions—whether this hurt or that hurt. They had all sorts of gadgets in the bag to examine him with.

At first they worked on him in a hurried, serious sort of way, calling out strange-sounding words and numbers. But then they changed their way somehow, and Toughboy and Sister looked at each other hopefully. Finally the tall soldier looked up and gave them a smile. It was a real smile, Toughboy was sure. Not the kind that was meant to trick them.

"You're going to be okay," the soldier said to Nelson. "Got a heart like a lion." He nodded his head at Nelson in an admiring way. "You're a tough old guy, sir."

Toughboy and Sister pressed their lips together so they wouldn't cry, or laugh either. Nelson was a tough old guy, and no one knew that better than they did.

While Toughboy snapped the traps, Sister packed up the extra food and their clothes. The soldiers were finished examining Nelson and were ready to take him to the helicopter. Nelson didn't want to be carried in the stretcher, but the soldiers told him it was an air force rule, so he agreed, grumbling all the while.

After they had lifted Nelson into the helicopter, the tall soldier helped Toughboy nail the plywood on the windows and lock the doors of the cabin and cache and outhouse, while Sister lifted Charlie and Mutt into the helicopter. Then they carried the boxes Sister had packed down the bank. The soldiers put the boxes inside the helicopter and tied them down with wide straps.

When they were ready to take off Sister leaned her head against the window of the helicopter. She could feel the throb of the engines through her whole body. She saw the camp robbers coming to the shelf for their breakfast. Would they be lonesome now? Would they be hungry?

Toughboy thought that a helicopter was lots more interesting than a small plane. It hung in the sky like a spider at the end of its thread. He didn't feel sick at all.

The pilot gave him a headset just like his own and that cut out the noise of the engine. He could hear the tower in Galena giving the pilot instructions.

Toughboy imagined that he was the pilot. The old Indian ways, the old prospectors' ways, everything old left his mind. He was dazzled by the shining instruments on the panel, the power of the engine, the pilot's sure ways.

He would go into the air force and be a helicopter pilot.

# 35

SISTER WAS STANDING IN THE BACK row, singing with the other children. They had to stand up so they could see over the heads of the children sitting in front of them. Only the children who didn't fool around were in the back row.

Sister's hair was braided so tightly her cheeks felt stiff.

They were singing her favorite song for Christmas, "O Little Town of Bethlehem." Bethlehem must have been a little village like theirs.

The teacher hadn't even asked to see the schoolwork they were supposed to do because she'd heard about the helicopter and all.

Sister felt guilty about that because she was pretty sure the teacher thought they'd left their schoolwork behind at the trapline when they were flown out.

She sure didn't know that they hadn't taken it at all.

On Christmas Day Natasha gave them a package that had come in the mail for them. It had their names on it. Annie Laurie Silas and John Silas.

They had never had a package in the mail before.

There was a record for Sister, "The Robert Shaw Chorale Sings Songs of Scotland." A list of the songs on the record was written on the back, and the first one on the list was "Annie Laurie."

Sister could hardly wait to listen to it on the record player at school.

There was a plastic model for Toughboy, one that you put together yourself. It was a model of a helicopter, the same kind they'd ridden in.

For Natasha there was a box of candy and two pairs of heavy wool socks. That was a joke, because Natasha had frozen her toes when she had to *siwash* in that bad cold. Nelson had pinned a note on the socks that said, "Next time, wear two pairs."

For Mutt there was a box of dog biscuits shaped like bones. Natasha said she and Mutt were two of a kind with their frozen feet. And she said they were both too tough to let a little thing like that slow them down any.

The letter from Nelson said he'd asked the nurse in the hospital to buy these things for him. He would come through their village on his way back to his claim to visit them. He was doing just fine.

He'd had an operation on his spleen, and if they didn't know what that was, they shouldn't feel bad. He didn't even know he had one until they'd operated on it.

Sister thought about how Natasha had wanted to teach them the old ways. Nelson thought the old ways were best, too.

But it was the new ways that had saved Nelson.

Maybe you should just take the good part of the old ways and the good part of the new ways and make your own way. Maybe that was what most people did, but they just didn't know it.